Dear Diary

The diaries of Lily Fox

A.K.A

Lady Elizabeth Caroline de Foix

Liz Hurley

First published 2019 by Mudlark's Press

This is a work of fiction. Names, characters, places, and incidents either are the product of the author's imagination or are used fictitiously. Any resemblance to actual persons, living or dead, events, or locales is entirely coincidental.

Copyright © 2019 by Liz Hurley

All rights reserved. No part of this book may be reproduced or used in any manner without written permission of the copyright owner except for the use of quotations in a book review.

First paperback edition 2020

ISBN 978-0-9932180-7-1
(paperback)

www.lizhurleywrites.com

:

DEDICATION

To teenagers everywhere, no matter how old we are.

CONTENTS

ACKNOWLEDGMENTS

Thank you to Spotify for hosting some fabulous playlists.

FOREWORD

I found my mother's diaries whilst I was rummaging around in the attic rooms. I have copied them out here, to share with my sisters. I know that we will all read and treasure them.

Clemmie

1 AUTUMN

Dear Diary,

New beginnings so a new diary. Picked this up in Jarrolds; typical isn't it? I trawled all over Norwich, had high hopes for the shops on Elm Hill but none were quite right, then I popped into Jarrolds and lo-and-behold this perfect diary. Sure, it's not the prettiest, but this reflects my new more serious outlook in taking control of my future. New me, new beginnings, new serious diary.

Anyway, what are these new beginnings? Well, I have only managed to finally convince Daddy to let me go to Art College! Lucinda's off to somewhere in Switzerland to learn to paint, whilst speaking French or something equally ridiculous. Honestly, when I think how stuffy my folks are, I thank my lucky stars that I don't have Lucy's parents. I mean seriously, finishing school? Who even does that anymore? Well, Lucy does, poor thing.

She thinks it will finish her off permanently! I don't know if her parents have really thought about the consequences of letting her loose on Switzerland though. They were neutral in the last war, I can't imagine them remaining neutral if Lucy fills their fountains with washing-up liquid. God that was funny, how she didn't get sent down none of us know. I reckon her father must have a filing cabinet full of incriminating photos of headmasters. Always thought she was for the high jump when she drew a moustache on the Virgin Mary in chapel. She might have got away with it if she hadn't signed it!!!

Quite a lot of the girls are off to university in order to get a husband, which I have to confess I'm really jealous about. And I can say that here because no one will ever know, but I so want to go to university.

I tried to use that as an excuse to Daddy, as to why I needed to go to uni, but he said I would get a husband the "normal" way and then harrumphed and refused to elucidate on what exactly the normal way was. I pointed out that arranged marriages were no longer a thing. Mummy mentioned a coming out party and I was so horrified by the notion that I skedaddled (is that how you spell it?) out of the room. I think that was pretty sneaky of Mummy; she knows I have no intention of getting married ever.

No, the reason why I am secretly jealous of the girls is that I would love to go to university. I know that makes me a bit of a swot but I really enjoyed school and learning stuff and the idea of going to a place where everyone wants to be there, and learning really great things, sounds so exciting. But not for me, oh no, I'm just a girl, educating girls past 18 is a waste of time. Educating David is a waste of time, if you ask me. He's going to inherit the estate and become Lord Hiverton so why does he even need a degree? Even he agrees, school wasn't really his thing. The way he talks about uni it just seems to be rowing, rugby, drinking and parties. And presumably girls. Girls looking for husbands. How funny if he fell for a bluestocking. Not that she'd have a bar of him. I don't think she'd be impressed by how many birds he can bag in a season and the arable yield of the lower fields.

He doesn't need uni for any of that, he already knows so much about running this estate, he's going to be brilliant at it. Apparently though, according to Mummy, he's going to Uni to get a broader outlook on life and make new connections. David mentioned something about sowing oats so I don't know if we have changed our crop rotations. Must make a note to ask Daddy about it and show him that I am interested in the estate.

But anyway, what does Daddy think I'm going to do with myself? I'm not going to get married and have children, he doesn't want me to get a degree, so what am I to do? Work?! I told him I was going to apply for a position in the local shoe shop and I swear his eye actually twitched. Then I said I was going to work in Africa with the nuns, helping little orphaned babies, and both his eyes twitched. Cue Mummy, pointing out that art school might be an acceptable solution for a year or two. Right, time for bed. My first diary entry has been a bit of a ramble but tomorrow, if nothing exciting happens, as if, I'll write more about my new college.

Dear Diary,

Nothing exciting happened today, well apparently, the village shop had run out of honey, so there's that piece of earth-shattering news from the epicentre of Norfolk (the buzzing metropolis that Hiverton is), but otherwise, nothing exciting.

So, ART COLLEGE!! It's this really beautiful building by the river and it is full of so many talented people. Honestly, they are incredible, I thought there's no way they'll want someone like me. I'm going to do a Performing Arts B-Tec, I'm telling Daddy it's an Arts degree; I think if I mentioned "performance" it would be game over. Not that I will be acting, I saw one of their plays and they were incredible. There's no way I'd ever be able to be anything like them, plus I'm not sure I'd feel very comfortable with people looking at me. Anyway, I get to pick and choose the strands I'm interested in. I feel like I'm in a sweet shop. The admissions officer was so lovely, he said that with my three As I was a bit over-qualified for the course so I had a bit of a panic, but a lack of a portfolio went against me a bit. Oh to have a portfolio! So I had a bit more of a panic.

Anyway, we went through the strands and together we picked Piano, Fashion, Architectural Studies, French and Photography. I can't wait to tell Lucy I'm basically going to Finishing School, but in Norwich, with boys and parties! Very excited! Mummy has been an absolute sport and given me money to buy all my course books so I've been reading through all of them ready for the start of term. Piano will obviously be a doddle, but I'm really looking forward to Photography. Daddy said he will consider lending me his Box Brownie. I tried to look grateful rather than appalled. I may have failed! I'm going to pinch David's, it's much newer.

Dear Diary,

Cycled over to Hever's to get some honey. They have also run out. This is getting serious. In other news… How can there be other news when honey levels are at an all-time low?

So basically no other news. Bit bored, decent weather, might go for a swim tomorrow.

Dear Diary,

This is getting silly. Went for a swim over at Blakeney, fabulous cycle ride over there. Swallows are beginning to bunch up on the lines, summer's almost over. Bought Mummy some honey from a local newsagent's and apparently I bought the honey that foreigners use to preserve dead bodies in hot weather. That doesn't sound right to me, but Mummy was deadly serious. I mean maybe they did in the past, and maybe they still do now, although it sounds a bit weird. Surely they don't then scrape the honey off the dead person and put it into jam jars? Anyway, it's been added to the village raffle. God forbid we should eat mummified honey.

Dear Diary,

Sorry, it's been a few days. The excitement of the honey wars has been hotting up. Mummy had to pop over to Somerlyton as Caroline has a glut.

Mummy was livid, honestly it's like the Archers around here, Caroline was so smug about how productive her bees are so now Mummy has sent her a bunch of flowers and a bottle of our award-winning cider in retaliation. I am awaiting the delivery of half a side of beef. Those two will out-do each other in "niceness" and kill and bankrupt us all in the process.

Dear Diary,

IT'S WAR. FULL ON WAR. John was chatting to Caroline's gardener trying to get tips as to why his hives are flourishing and ours are a little quiet and you'll never guess what? His hives are also quiet. Caroline only went out and bought Dead Man's honey and RE-LABELLED it!!!! Oh my God. Mummy exploded. Daddy thought it was a poor show on Caroline's behalf but has also, wisely, decided not to get involved. Which is fuelling Mummy's fury. I find that I am cycling, a lot.

Dear Diary,

College tomorrow. Can't write anything else, too excited.

Dear Diary,

Oh wow. College is incredible, I am so lucky, but it does all feel very weird. Didn't speak to anyone, smiled at a few people but everyone seemed to know everyone else and they were all so loud. The energy is incredible, but I was a bit overwhelmed. I think I'll just be happy to sit back and watch for a bit. The lessons were really rowdy, and I was a bit shocked by the lack of discipline but realise I sound a bit like Daddy. So, need to stop that. Right now. I bet it will calm down tomorrow. So many boys here. Daunting.

Dear Diary,

It didn't calm down. I tell you it's all a bit of a shock. All our tutors go by their first names which seems really weird. Nice boy smiled at me. I smiled back. I know he's nice because he smiled at me! Plus he looks like an Italian angel. He has almost black hair, in big thick curls. Daddy would say it needs a good cut! Still haven't talked to anyone. Missed Architecture, couldn't find the damned building. Felt like a total first year. Which I am, but you know. I don't like the bus journey, it's long and the seat fabric makes the back of my legs prickle. I came home late yesterday and didn't get in until seven and the parents were about to call out the national guard. Long story short, I'm having Mummy's mini and she's getting a new car. David will be livid! Win win.

Dear Diary,

Week One completed. I love Piano. Obviously. But it's really nice to just go and have the time to go and unwind and just let it all out on the ivories. Been doing duets which was really exciting and I have to compose a few pieces in the style of a composer of my choice. Then the rest of the class have to guess who each of us were inspired by. That's going to be fun. I think I'm going to cheat and go with Chopin, he's so distinctive. Still, I bet everyone will think the same. Maybe Debussy? Maybe chopsticks?

Photography is amazing and I think that's

already my favourite. I can't paint for tuppence but this is a way that I can sort of present a picture of what I'm seeing. I have a reel of film and I have to take pictures of "Happy" and then next week we will actually learn how to develop our own pictures in a dark room! We're working in black and white but Gary, that's our lecturer (still weird calling one of the master's Gary), he says that working in black and white strips the picture down to its raw parts. So "Happy" in its raw features. Bit stumped because, for example, seeing a poppy makes me happy but a huge part of what makes me happy is the lovely colour of red against the sandy curbs and the yellow cornfields. Maybe I should just take photos of Bella?

French was good, it's actually nice to have a normal lesson. Struggling with some of the past-historical. There was a poster in the corridor for Russian and I am going to investigate that on Monday. It did say it was a beginner's class.

Architectural Studies. Well, I suppose it couldn't all be good news. Mr Houlihan, Mr Houlihan doesn't believe in first names and now I'm conflicted; neither did I until I found myself on the same side of the fence as him, hateful man. Anyway, Mr Houlihan was really rude to me and it felt really unfair. As you know I missed the first lesson, and then I was a bit late for the second lesson. I had already found where the room was the day before, so I wouldn't be late next time. Clever hey? But then just before the lesson I had to help someone find the canteen, and it was really nice to be able to say "Yes I can help with that" as opposed to looking like a bewildered sheep all week. So, anyway, a bit late, and I creep in really quietly, and he stops the lesson to ask who I am and why am I late? Like a little child! So I apologise and explain why I was just five minutes late, and he says "Well Miss Lah-di-dah, I don't appreciate students that can't be bothered to be punctual, if you are late again please don't bother opening the door. Ever again."!!!!! I was mortified.

Miss Lah-di-bloody-dah. And someone sniggered! I was so careful when I registered to make sure my title didn't go anywhere on the forms. Instead of Lady Elizabeth Caroline de Foix, I registered as Lily Fox, like a secret identity. I thought Lilibet was probably a bit babyish, but I needed to pick a name I would actually remember and reply to! And I still get name-called. I didn't catch much of the rest of the lesson as I was so busy veering between fury and embarrassment. The nice boy that smiled at me on day one was also in the class. He smiled at me again and made a rude gesture behind Mr Houlihan's back. It was very rude but cheered me up no end.

Fashion was amazing. Of course. Lots of really exciting stuff, not like Mummy's gowns at all. Neon and punk seem to be quite the thing. Not convinced, but gosh it is vibrant. Am keeping very quiet about Mummy's gowns. And Grandmama's.

Next week determined to actually talk to someone. Beginning to feel a bit like a ghost passing through groups of friends.

Dear Diary,

This weekend has been miserable, I'm really worried about Architecture tomorrow. I know it's silly, but it's been really tough to take photos of "Happy" when I'm feeling so bad. Mummy noticed I was a bit quiet and has suggested that we go out for tea after college tomorrow so I'm going to take the bus in and Mummy will drive us home. Tomorrow's task is to speak to someone.

Dear Diary,

Woo-hoo! Happy Monday! Someone spoke to me and I spoke back, so okay I didn't start it but it was a proper conversation and I have Horrid Houlihan to thank for it. I was in the canteen flicking through the College prospectus to see what other courses there are, when this girl came up to me and asked if I was the one late into Houlihan's lesson? Then she said he was completely out of order for behaving like that. Then some of her friends joined us and we had a great lunch chatting and laughing. Turns out they don't all know each other after all, they just act that way. Anyway, it made me feel really welcome and while they were laughing, I asked if I could take some photos of them for my homework and they were really up for it. I think I got some great shots. So anyway, that was brilliant and as I was taking pictures, the nice smiling boy came over. Turns out he went to sixth form with one of the girls so he said Hi. He called Houlihan even ruder names and I felt VERY happy.

Then when I was having tea with Mummy in the Waffle House, I told her about what Mr Houlihan had said and she was really supportive. She helped me get it into perspective, and I have to confess I was beginning to let it get out of control, but she also supported my decision to switch classes. After all, unless my heart is set on Architectural Studies why stick with a tutor that you can't respect? Honestly, just when you think you are all grown up and standing on your own two feet, it's Mummy to the rescue. She thinks History of Art sounds really interesting as well, so I will go and visit the admission office tomorrow to see if I can swap things over.

Best of all, when I got home there was a letter from David! It wasn't a very long letter, but it was really lovely to "hear" his voice. He's decided he's actually going to do some work this year as it's his final year, he reckons he'll be lucky to scrape a Tutu; that's uni speak for a lower second degree, he's also been made head of the Rowing Sevens so he's elated as that is far more important. Of course.

Dear Diary,

Went into college really early today. Didn't want to drive in the rush hour, Norwich is so busy, but I overdid it and arrived at 8 a.m. Still, the offices were open and I have now swapped over to History of Art. The Secretary asked if I was the student that Mr Houlihan had singled out. I said I didn't know what she was talking about because I didn't want to make matters worse but how did she know? Did someone complain? Wow! It's really silly but when I heard someone snigger, it was almost as crushing as his rude name calling.

Anyway, History of Art is fascinating. We're looking at Greek pots at the moment, and did you know all their lovely white temples were once covered in bright paint, like red and green and blue. How amazing is that?

Went into Body Shop and got some dewberry shampoo. Smell is heavenly.

Dear Diary,

I seem to be getting the hang of College now, made some friends. Bit disappointed that nice boy, or Mikey, actually it's Michael but apparently that gets shortened to Mikey, not sure why. I prefer Michael. Anyway, like I was saying before I so rudely interrupted myself, I was a bit disappointed that he wouldn't be in my class any longer but then I walked into Russian, and there he was, and his face really lit up when he saw me, and he pulled out the chair next to him! He's got the most amazing voice. He's Irish, so he has this really lovely accent and his voice is really deep and he speaks really softly. So you sort of have to lean in to hear what he's saying. Well, that's my excuse anyway!

Michael is really interesting, I laugh loads when I'm with him. In fact, we both make each other laugh a lot. Sometimes it's because we both like the same things, other times it's because we do things that the other finds odd. For instance, the other day he bought chips from the market and walked through the streets eating them. He thought I was being really funny for being dubious about it. But he convinced me to do it as well, and no Mummy, the world did not stop turning! I don't think I'll do it again though, I gave myself indigestion. Look at me. Living life on the edge, eating in the street!

Dear Diary,

Michael made me a mix tape! There's some really good stuff, but a lot of it is also sad or angry. Honestly, I think the happy songs are just there to keep me listening. A lot of it is just noisy but the lyrics are really interesting. There's one called Teenage Kicks, which just seems to shout a lot but the words are great. I was playing it the other night and Mummy brought me some headache tablets. She said I was going to need them if I kept listening to that music. She also told me to make sure Daddy didn't hear it. Daddy has very strong opinions about punks. Tried to tell Mummy this wasn't punk music. She said it sounded like punk to her. Honestly, my folks are so old. Michael says he doesn't know much classical stuff, other than hymns, so I'm going to do him an upbeat classical mix tape. I might also try and sneak a few pop tunes through, see if I can make him wince :D

Dear Diary,

Off this weekend to Jilly's. It's her 19th. Can't believe we are so old. Any minute now we won't be teenagers anymore. I feel like I'm running out of time. I don't know for what but I just feel that life is screaming past me and I haven't done anything. Really looking forward to catching up with everyone, some of the girls are coming back from uni. Of course Lucy is still locked up in Switzerland. Am going to take my camera.

Dear Diary,

What a weekend, I am completely fagged. David was there which was a total surprise, he and a group of pals all came up from Bath. It was brilliant to see him, I really miss him these days. It was so funny, when he saw me he nearly freaked, I think he and Daddy both think I'm still ten. I was chatting to all his friends, but he kept spoiling things being heavy-handed and reminding them that I was his little sister. Honestly, he can be a right old fuddy-duddy. Claire and I built an awesome champagne tower and got it to flow properly and best of all no one knocked it over. The boys decided to play tug of war and Billy's team won, but they broke a side table and Jilly was really cross because she'd told them to do it outside. Clem and Mark got back together. Again! No doubt it will implode again soon in a total drama fest. There was quite a lot making out, I might have got lucky but David pretty much scared everyone off. I kept thinking of Michael but that made me feel bad because I don't think he'd like my friends much. He's a bit serious about stuff. And I don't like the idea of him looking down his nose at my friends.

He has a lot of opinions about everything. God, I make him sound awful and he's really not. He's so kind and caring but the other day he was complaining about some bigwig businessman crushing his workers, and then I realised he was talking about Anthony Fairweather's father. It was really awkward, I wanted to defend Mr Fairweather but I don't know anything about his business, just that Anthony's father plays a mean game of charades at Christmas and always gives me an extra dollop of cream with my strawberries at tennis. It's all very confusing. I'm beginning to feel like an observer whenever I'm out with either group of friends.

Dear Diary,

My photos are excellent. I'm making lots of copies and sending them to the girls. I got a really sweet one of Clem and Mark so I'm going to send them that one to remind them of just how good they are together. My tutor said I was really good at observing people, he suggested I was losing a bit of focus as the evening wore on. I think he was teasing me.

Dear Diary,

Tried a cigarette to blend in. Choked and my mascara ran down my face. Failed to blend in.

Dear Diary,

Sod blending in. Excuse rude language but I can't be anything that I'm not. What I can do though is keep my head down. I know I'm a chicken but everyone at college seems so political. They always seem to be angry about things. But they don't seem sad, they seem to enjoy being angry. Just when I think they are being annoying I remember that they are fighting for people that don't have a voice, which is really nice of them. I said this to Mummy, and she said we live in a democracy and that everyone has a voice. And she's right, so I just got more confused and told her they were arguing for better rights for women worldwide and anti-apartheid in South Africa which is really an awful thing. Mummy agreed it was terrible, but it was up to their own governments to sort things out. I'm pretty sure some of my new friends would have had an answer to that. Mummy suggested I didn't talk to Daddy about stuff like this. As if! I'm confused not suicidal.

Dear Diary,

Stinking cold, sore throat, look like a ghoul. Obviously, the first person I see is Michael. He said, "Morning Snotty." I want to die. Didn't see him for the rest of the day.

Dear Diary,

Beat Michael in a discussion about Russian history today. He was banging on about how fabulous the revolution had been in freeing the serfs. I pointed out that the Romanovs and the millions that died probably didn't see it the same way. He said I had my figures wrong and Marsha, our teacher, stepped in and said that I was probably being conservative with the figures. One of the many things that the Soviet era vigorously suppresses is accurate and open reporting. I think Michael was a bit surprised because he's used to people agreeing with him. Especially girls. Girls like Debbie. I'm beginning to think she hasn't a single thought that's her own. Debbie's one of Kim's friends, she's doing Fashion Design so of course she's very into ruffles and rips right now, she says they are the next big thing. I think she looks like a pirate. I don't think she likes me much. I think the feeling is reciprocated.

We were talking A-Level grades at lunch (everyone else calls it dinner – I wonder if different groups use different words for the same things, just to make outsiders uncomfortable or just so that they can be quickly identified? That's me off on a tangent about totalitarian societies. Back on track Lilibet). So, A-Level grades, and it turns out I have the best, by miles. Well, Michael grinned and said, "That's my girl" which gave me such a buzz but my stupid mouth opens up and I say, "I'm not your girl!" and Kim hooted and said, "That'll teach you, Michael!" and "Right on Sister" to me and gave me a salute. It was quite fun, suddenly I was a feminist, and a bluestocking too. No one knew what a bluestocking was, so I told them and then they were surprised to hear that there were upper-class feminists. I was surprised that they didn't know who Emmeline Pankhurst was. Sometimes I am very glad for my single-sex education, we seem to have been taught more about women than in mixed ed. schools or in the boys' schools.

Anyway, despite the ribbing, Michael seemed to take it on the chin and apologised for calling me "his". And I said I didn't really mind it and he said what, saying it or being it? And then he smiled at me really shyly and walked off!!!!!!

Was he asking me to be his girlfriend?

Dear Diary,

Michael wasn't in college today. Bought a new lip gloss. I spent every lesson looking out for him. Want to die. This feels rubbish.

Dear Diary,

Michael was waiting for me in the student car park. He looked really pleased to see me. I tried to be cool, but I was grinning too much and then he hugged me and said he'd missed me yesterday and I nearly died! So happy.

Am currently reading a book he gave me called Animal Farm. He was surprised I knew so much about Russian history but had never heard of George Orwell. Not sure if it will be very good as Daddy never mentioned Orwell, and he's quite hot on his history. It's one of the things we like talking about. Not sure about this book, I think it's a children's book. Maybe it meant something to Michael growing up?

Dear Diary,

Sunday evening. Two things. One. Wow. Two. Oh my God, WOW!

One. Michael had inscribed the book to "My Blue Stocking, if I may be so bold!" He is so clever and nice and really very confusing. Are we dating? Does he want to ask me out? Has he asked me out? Have I got a boyfriend and I don't know!? SO CONFUSED. Very, very happy and excited. God, I hope I'm not over-interpreting things and he's like this with everyone.

Two. George Orwell is incredible. Finished Animal Farm. It is incredible. Am heading straight into the library tomorrow to borrow everything else he has ever written.

Dear Diary,

Spent ages picking out what to wear today, got stuck in the rush hour traffic, missed Russian, didn't see Michael as he had to leave early for a dentist's appointment, apparently. Gutted.

Dear Diary,

How have I never heard of George Orwell? His writing is so clean but so powerful. I always thought I knew both sides of the arguments in history. I'm beginning to think I may know both sides, but I have learnt both sides from only one of those sides. It would be like Hitler explaining the War from the Allies' point of view. Feeling a bit stupid for realising that the other side may not interpret events in the same way. Eye opening. Love my new lip gloss, tastes of cherry.

Dear Diary,

It's Official. I have a boyfriend and I am so lucky because I feel like I'm dating my best friend. We went for a coffee after college and he suggested we go and watch a movie and we talked so much we totally missed the start! Then at the end he said he'd had fun and we should do this again tomorrow. And I joked that people would talk. And he said let them, it would make his day. Then his bus arrived and just before he jumped on it he said, "Goodnight girlfriend" and kissed me! And before I could do anything he jumped on the bus and I stood there grinning like a fool. It wasn't a proper kiss or anything, just a quick kiss, but it was on the lips!

Dear Diary,

Sorry, it's been a while but I've been having so much fun and now Michael and me have had a huge row over something really stupid and I don't know if we are even going out anymore. I don't think I have ever been so miserable.

To be continued…

Mix Tape for Lily

https://open.spotify.com/playlist/1m1WecSLF1nw6cqKA45ZLt

Songs for the Arch Angel Michael

https://open.spotify.com/playlist/6NympsemD1mZWOvuwhLtoR

2 WINTER

Dear Diary,

Sorry. Couldn't write anything else yesterday. I feel so sick. Haven't gone into College now for two days. I just drive into Norwich and then sit in the city library all day and read and do my homework. Terrified that someone will see me and report me. Which is silly because who cares?

No one cares. No one cares about anything.

For the past month Michael and I have been dating, and it's been brilliant. We've only kissed, and that's been great. He hasn't pressurised me for anything else and in fact one time I got a bit carried away and he said no. I laughed and then he did as well. I said it's not normally the boy who says no, and he smiled so sweetly and said I was worth waiting for. I swear I nearly died on the spot. How many boys talk like that?

And he's been true to his word, even when we both get a bit carried away he always says stop. He laughs that I'm killing him. So we just hold hands and kiss and stuff, but it's been really great because I don't feel any pressure, even if I am too old to still be a virgin.

And then we had a stupid row, and he told me I didn't know what I was talking about and I was naïve and stupid and stuck-up. And I shouted at him and started crying because I don't mean to be stuck-up and I try not to be stupid but I can't do much about being naïve because I haven't grown up like him.

It all started the day before when I was walking into college and two drunk tramps shouted out at me and told me I had nice tits and they'd like to give me one. One of them chased after me and I'm certain that he only did it to scare me, he wouldn't actually have done anything, I mean God he was drunk and at 9 a.m. But it did scare me. It scared me a bloody lot, actually. Anyway, I didn't tell anyone because I didn't want to make a big thing of it. Plus I thought if I had to tell anyone I might start crying and that would spoil everything I am trying to project about being independent and grown-up. Lily Fox doesn't blub at scary men, she laughs and calls them losers. However, Elizabeth de Foix walked the long way home to her car at the end of the day and then drove home, crying all the way.

So, the following day I drove into college and parked on the other side of town and walked in from the other direction. After Russian Michael and I walked into town, to look through the record shops.

Well, just as we crossed the bridge the two tramps from yesterday were sat in a doorway drinking. They didn't even look up at us as we walked towards them, but I was still a bit freaked so I stepped to the other side of Michael and muttered that they were revolting. Michael stopped talking and when we were out of sight of them he stopped and asked me what I meant?

And then he just sort of went off on a total rage. He asked me if I had ever slept on the streets before and I laughed because it was such a funny idea but told him once after the Snow Ball we had almost fallen asleep in the hotel pavilion. I don't know why I said that, but I was nervous and trying to make him laugh because he suddenly seemed really angry at me. And then it just seemed to get out of control. It didn't make him laugh at all. He kept shouting at me about how horrible and scary it is having to live on the streets and then I realised that he must have done it which was really shocking. And I tried to apologise and explain what they had done the day before but I didn't get far before he started shouting that when your life is that miserable, maybe I too would want to drink to forget about it.

So he's shouting at me and I'm trying not to cry and trying to get him to hear what I'm trying to say and then things got ten times worse. This really nice policeman came over and asked if everything was OK, and I tried to explain that we were having a small misunderstanding and then Michael told him to push off and then the policeman went from being nice and kind to suddenly looking really quite cross. It all seemed to get out of control and I figured that the only way to stop it getting worse was to walk away. So

I did. And that was two days ago. I'm going to have to go back in tomorrow and just get it over with.

Mummy knows something is up, she got Cook to make chocolate mousse as a special treat. She only does that when things are either really good or really bad. Didn't eat it. Feel sick.

Dear Diary,

I'm on cloud ten. Much better than cloud nine. I decided to park in my normal spot, I can't be scared (well I can but I have to try and face up to the things that scare me, plus I had a bottle of mace in my bag and a rape alarm, and one of Daddy's fishing knives. Total overkill but it made me feel good) Anyway as I pulled up I saw Michael leaning on the wall. When he saw me he ran over to me and as I got out of the car, he kept hugging me and telling me he was a fool and that he was so sorry. Then he started crying saying that I was the best thing that had ever happened to him and he was an idiot and had got scared that I would leave him if I ever found out that he had slept on the streets. Like I would ever care.

So after a lot of kissing and crying, we promised never to argue again. And I finally got to explain what had actually happened. Michael got really quiet at that point and I thought he was even crosser than last time. Holding my hand he walked me all the way to the admin office and told the staff that he wanted to register a formal complaint about me being intimidated and we were taken straight into the College Director's office and it turns out I'm not the first person this had happened to. The police had been called yesterday and had had words with them. The

Director asked if I wanted to add my name to a formal complaint but I said no. Can you imagine it? Mummy and Daddy would have me out of there in an instant. And anyway I said I had come in with protection so I wasn't scared anymore and when I showed them the knife and the mace and the alarm, I think they were rather startled.

Michael looked at me like he hadn't seen me before and also looked really ashamed. He says I'm the bravest person he knows, which is stupid given that he has had to sleep on the streets. I don't know what happened there. I'll ask when everything has calmed down. It's obviously something that upsets him greatly. Well dur.

Dear Diary,

The last few days have been a happy blur. Went to a bonfire and fireworks display at Mousehold Heath. It was fabulous, we could see the whole city lit up by fireworks. Michael said the fireworks were like his heart exploding every time he sees me. Bright and fizzy and happy. Champagne fireworks. I don't know about exploding but my heart melted. He says the most beautiful things. It was so wonderful standing in the crowd with his arms around me as we watched the skies and the flames. I felt like we were the only two people in the whole world. Even with everyone else there. That's how he makes me feel. As soon as I see him everyone else fades away. There is only him in the whole universe.

Dear Diary,

Just been reading over the past few weeks and

I have noticed two things. Firstly, I'm not very good at writing daily and secondly, all I seem to write about is Michael. And whilst he is not boring I don't want to be one of those boring girls that can only talk about their boyfriend. Of course, other things have been happening as well. In fact some of them quite earth-shattering. Mrs Parker Thompson has finally resigned her position as First Soprano. I know! Drum roll. So anyway last night in Choir practice Mummy and Caroline start discussing who should take her place. Clearly, they both want the position but wouldn't dream of actually putting themselves forward. And quite frankly Caroline can't carry a tune in a bucket. Anyway, I started doodling because it was so boring and I decided to see how many words I could make out of M I C H A E L. Not too many as it happens, so I added his surname B Y R NE and got a few more. Then I decided to see how many French words I could get and upped my word count again. Then I decided to see if I could manage anything in Russian and of course, first I had to transpose the alphabet. Told you I was bored. Anyway, right in the middle of Михаил, I hear Mummy say my name, and when I look up everyone is looking at me and nodding. It was no good, everyone was in agreement, and what they agreed was that they didn't care that I had said no. Quite emphatically. Many times.

So, tada. I am First Soprano. I was promised I wouldn't have to do any solos. Which made me feel better. So I sort of agreed I'd consider it. Which was taken as yes. Then it turned out that no solos meant no solos except for the few solo bits. Which basically just means leading one or two carols as the soloist before the others join in a few bars behind. So solos, then.

Have written to David to see if he can persuade Mummy to let me off the hook.

Dear Diary,

Told Michael all about it and he said it sounds fab and can he come and listen. This is getting out of hand. There is no way I am letting him see me in the Hyssop Singers choral gowns. They are made of nylon and look like something the Beatles would have worn when they were in India. Personally, I think the committee must have been a little bit down the sherry bottle when they came up with the design. Mummy says they are "jolly" but she also threatened to resign when they were revealed. She also wears a cotton slip under them. Poor Mummy, wearing nylon. How she suffers :D

Anyway told Michael I was trying to get David onside to help get me out of it. So there's no point in him coming anyway.

I realise I am also putting this off. Neither of us speaks about our families. Obviously, I won't meet his for ages, being in Ireland and all that, but mine are literally just up the road. It's just. I'm not ashamed or embarrassed about my family. It's just, I'm beginning to realise that they may be a little overwhelming. And I really don't want to put Michael off me.

Dear Diary,

Got a letter from David today. It said, "Ha ha. No way. Remember when I had to be lead chorister and my voice broke during the first verse of Once in Royal and you laughed?" Hmm. They say no good deed goes unpunished and apparently neither does a bad deed. Damn.

Hark the bloody heralds, it is then.

Also wrote back and apologised. That was ten years ago. Talk about holding a grudge. At this rate, he'll suggest the church install spotlights.

Dear Diary,

Got some of my papers marked from before half term. Really pleased with the results. I was a bit worried that they might be worse as I know I'm a bit distracted by Michael. A bit!

Chatting with Zandi (that's how it's spelt, I know, she scribbles her name everywhere – like she's trying to remember it (I recognise the signs!)) (oh look – double bracket closure ;D) Anyway, Zandi in Fashion. I told her about this awful dress issue and she told me to bring a photo in to see if she could make any suggestions. Have found one from the drinks party afterwards so will show her tomorrow.

Dear Diary,

Showed Zandi the photo. Two things. First, she laughed her head off. Second, she said I really was a little posh girl. The only picture I could find was in the Flint-Hyssops ballroom. I had to snatch the photo out of her hand as she was threatening to pass it around the class. I might have sulked a bit because she apologised and said I couldn't help where I was born. Which is true. And she also said that few people had to suffer like I did if I had to wear that dress in public. Also true. Anyway, she's going to think about it over the weekend.

Dear Diary,

Great choir session. I mean I love singing, my previous comments probably didn't make that clear but I just don't want people looking at me. I'd rather be singing from behind the piano or handing out mince pies. Anyway, good rehearsal. Caroline was lovely about my voice and only made four or five suggestions as to how I could improve it. Honestly, I don't know why Mummy is friends with her, she's impossible. Miss Feathers and Miss Flight (aren't they fabulous names?) were also really nice, and they were actually nice as opposed to Caroline nice. The two Fs live in Saxburgh and share a house. Apparently, it's cheaper that way as neither of them ever found a husband. I'm glad they have company, they are both really lovely, they are always involved in the church and always send knitted blankets to little babies in Africa.

David said they were gay, and I agreed that they were really nice and he laughed at me and said they were lesbians. Since when did gay mean lesbian? Have I been using it improperly all this time? Mummy referred to the window display in Laura Ashley as gay the other day. Surely she didn't mean to say that Laura Ashley is for lesbians? And out loud. Can't see Mummy approving of that sort of thing. Don't know who to ask. Don't want to look like a total idiot. I don't care about people being lesbians, I mean who cares, as long as you are happy and not hurting anyone, but I do care about looking stupid.

Hope Zandi has a solution for the dress.

Dear Diary,

Gorgeous Sunday. Did nothing all day long.

Dear Diary,

Zandi's solutions are all a bit extreme. I don't think she's quite understood how terrifying the choirmaster is. Solutions that won't work include cutting it short, dyeing it, adding ruffles, or zips. Zandi definitely thinks zips and ruffles are the solution to everything. Then she started tripping and suggested that as lead singer I should stand out and wear a dress that was just one colour. Same awful shape, bell sleeves and high crimped neck, but just in a simple colour picking out one of the colours in the other dresses. Or maybe add a small trim on the cuffs and collar made in the other fabric. It's actually a really smart idea. The only problem is that it draws more attention to me not less.

Dear Diary,

Went to the cinema after college with Michael and then we drove up to Zaks for a burger and watched the city lights.

Finally had the parents talk. I think because it was dark it was easier for Michael. I can't believe how much he has suffered and is still so incredible, I don't think I'd be anywhere as nice as him. Michael doesn't have any parents. At least he doesn't know them. They could be dead or alive. He was given over to the nuns in Ireland as a little baby and then he spent his life living in children's homes and foster families. He said it wasn't terrible, and he knows that for some kids it really was incredibly awful. He said some of the priests were perverts but that didn't make sense and he was so angry about it, I could feel him shaking beside me, that I didn't dare ask. For him, though, he said it was just mostly lonely. Children would come and go. You couldn't make friends for any length of time. Sometimes he would be shipped off to another town and have to start again in a new family. He moved constantly. Sometimes he would run away back to one particular children's home where he had a favourite nun. He laughed about it but it didn't sound very funny. When he was 16, he got a job and then hitchhiked over to England. He was going to carry on working but a social worker found him sleeping on the streets and got him into school.

He asked me about mine and said that I had seemed scared of Daddy finding out about those tramps and he asked if Daddy hit me! I was stunned. How could he even think that?

I mumbled that my folks were nice but boring and strict and old-fashioned. How could I say anything else?

Dropped him back at his bedsit and cried the whole way home thinking of him as a little boy. I am going to make sure he has the best Christmas ever.

Dear Diary,

I'm an idiot. I was so shocked that Michael would think Daddy hits me, that I couldn't stop thinking about it and then it finally dawned on me. Of course he would think that because for him he had seen it before. He must have grown up seeing men hit children. Can't stop crying.

Dear Diary,

Am making Michael a Christmas Mix Tape. Will also get him a Led Zeppelin album. He said he really liked it on the mix tape I did him. I'm tempted to get him the new ABBA one as well, just to see his face! I don't think I can make a fan of him :D Also buying him some painting brushes and a new roll for his brushes. His current one is more sellotape and staples holding it together. Going to make him a stocking as he said he's never had one before. I'm also giving him an advent calendar kiss for every day, in the post. The Sunday one will be in an envelope in the Saturday one with a "Do Not Open Until Sunday" warning.

Dear Diary,

Yippee, Daddy has finally relented and put the heating on. It's lovely down in the sitting rooms where the fires are lit and of course the kitchen has the Aga and whilst I do have a little fire burning in my bedroom it goes out quite quickly. But the rest of the house I have to sprint along freezing corridors and hallways and the loo seats are freezing. The only warm loo in the whole damn house is the one downstairs behind the wall where the Aga sits. It just takes so long to get to it and everywhere is freezing and I always wake up the dogs. Daddy says they should be out in the kennels but Mummy insists they sleep indoors. I can see my breath in front of me and yesterday I showed Mummy the ice on the inside of my window.

The central heating is a bit hit and miss, and bangs and clanks a lot but at least now I don't have to sleep with tomorrow's clothes in bed with me!

Dear Diary,

Michael thinks I'm nuts because I keep asking him when his postman delivers. Happily, it's before college so I am going to post his first kiss and then he'll have it before we meet up in college. And then I suppose I'll just have to give him a bonus kiss. What a hardship. Can't wait to surprise him. Also going to ask Mummy if Michael can come for Christmas. Apparently, David is bringing Cecily, and there'll be lots of people coming and going so another mouth to feed shouldn't be an issue. Not going to say anything to Michael. Cecily is so boring and really stupid. I can't see why David likes her. I was really hoping they'd have split up by now. Mummy likes her as well and says she's the right sort. I hope she can see that Michael is the right sort. Even if he isn't because he is, really. He's the rightest sort there is.

Dear Diary,

Bloody hell. New curate has introduced some new carols to be accompanied by guitars and tambourine. We have become hippies. Apparently, I would embrace this because I'm young. I'm young not tone deaf. Or weird. Other than that practice went well, I love the descant lines. There's also one glorious carol where me and James (lead bass) sing a lovely call and refrain. I haven't heard it before but I'm in love with it. There's also a gorgeous song called Gaudete. Loads of harmonies which the local primary school is doing. They will progress in single file, each holding a candle. Tears ahead!

Dear Diary,

Great day with Michael. We both have a free first and second so we always go for coffee at the local café.

Dear Diary,

I am still blushing. Russian first thing and no Michael. I was really upset because today's the first and I was really hoping he would have got my first lipstick advent kiss. Anyway, Miss was in the middle of explaining the concept of colours, they see blue as two distinctly named different colours. Say like navy and well, we don't have a name for pale blue do we, but we still say navy is a shade of blue. But they call it a different colour. A bit like pink I suppose, that really is a shade of red but we never think that, we view that as a different colour, not just a name for a shade of red. It was really interesting and hard to get my head around. Anyway, back on track. The door opens and Michael comes in apologising to Miss and then walks straight over to me and gives me a huge kiss in front of the whole class. Everyone was cheering and laughing and I could have died. It was so romantic and so embarrassing. Miss was really sweet and said that whilst high drama was very much in the Russian tradition, could he save it for after the lesson? I went every single shade of red, from hot and bothered to tickled pink.

Turns out he was late waiting for the postman to see what I was up to. And then of course when he got the kiss he then ran into college so that he could see me. He ran all the way!

And then the best bit of news, Mummy said he

was welcome to join us for Christmas. I think they are very curious about him; I haven't told them anything because I don't think they'd understand. They just know we go to college together, that he's called Michael and that I think he's the best thing ever. Daddy says he'll be sleeping in the garden wing. He also made a "joke" about sleeping in the corridor. Daddy, not Michael. I only know that's a joke because Daddy would never rough it. A bear trap would be more likely. Can't wait to invite Michael. Super excited.

Dear Diary,

Well, today didn't exactly go according to plan. I got all excited and told Michael all about it after he returned my advent kiss. I love that! And he said could he think about it? I have to be honest that really hurt me, I just don't understand why he hasn't said yes. It will be fabulous and we can be together over Christmas, and he's never had a proper Christmas. Now it's the weekend so I won't hear from him until Monday. I tried calling the phone box on his street on the off chance that he'd be passing. Obviously he wasn't, and some girl told me to get off the line as she was waiting for a call. Michael and I hadn't arranged a time. In fact, I think he might be about to call it all off. I don't know what I've done wrong. He loved the advent kisses so much so I don't think it's that. Maybe I'm being too suffocating? I didn't think I was but David said that girls that chase after boys are the worst and the easiest. And that I should never do that. Have I been chasing?

Dear Diary,

Rubbish weekend. Baked decorations for the tree with Cook, helped dress the house, choir practice went well. Although one of the school children is a total prima donna and has asked if she can wear a special robe, to mark her out as the lead singer. She's not even that good a singer, but her father sells lots of cars and she has very pretty blonde curls, so she looks really angelic leading the children down through the church aisle.

Watched Sound of Music with the folks. Dogs gently snoring in front of the fire. Should have been lovely, but I felt sick to my stomach. What have I done wrong?

Dear Diary,

No Michael in college today. Went to his house. He shares it with a bunch of other people and honestly, it smells a bit. No one had seen him since Sunday. What does this mean? Has he gone away? Has he left college? Surely he would tell me? When they opened the door, I could see two envelopes from me on the floor with the other unopened mail. I feel dumped and discarded. I asked the man called Baz to let him know I had called.

Dear Diary,

Still no Michael. Went to his place again. Now three letters from me on the floor. One of the envelopes had a boot mark on it where someone had walked over it. Didn't leave a message, what's the point? Mummy asked if I had a confirmation yet and I started shouting at her which really isn't like me. Then Daddy came in and shouted at me and I shouted back which as I said isn't like me, and then I got sent to my bedroom like an eight-year-old.

Dear Diary,

Housekeeper told Daddy that we are being plagued by nuisance calls, someone with a silly accent calling for someone called Lily. Apparently, they have reported it to British Telecoms. So excited but don't know quite how to approach the problem. When Daddy was out, I found Mrs H and told her what I thought might have happened. He's been calling all week sounding more and more exasperated. Of course, he doesn't know I'm operating under a different name and I haven't told anyone in the house that he's Irish. Easy mistake. Mrs H said if he called again she would come and find me or take a message. Gave her a huge hug.

Dear Diary,

All fixed. Well sort of but I've been a real idiot. I mean a prize idiot. I would win an Oscar for how big an idiot I've been. Here's what happened.

Michael came back to college, apparently he'd taken off for a few days to think things through because, for him, me asking him was a big deal. He says he has never felt this way about anyone before and it scares him. He was deciding if he was all in or going to bail completely!!! This made me cry. I didn't know my future was being decided by him, without any input from me. And all because I invited him for Christmas. How was I supposed to argue the case for us, if I didn't know that "us" was in jeopardy? Anyway that was when the penny had dropped and I realised that he was making a decision about us, based on a lie. My lie. Like I said. Idiot.

So then I had to tell him my real name and where I live. The whole thing. I felt awful. And do you know what he did? My gorgeous, wonderful, adorable Michael burst out laughing. In fact, he was laughing so hard he fell off his chair. Then he told me he always knew I was a princess and then laughed some more. He asked if I actually knew any princesses, so I said of course not. Well, not any British ones anyway. There was a Saudi one at school and I got a letter from Lucy the other day where she said there were so many princesses at the finishing school that the rarest title was Miss. I told Michael that and he laughed some more. I think it was a touch hysterical. I had to keep telling him my family were going to love him but he said it didn't matter he had already decided. He was all in.

I tried to explain to him why I'd lied about my name. People are always judging me because I have a title and because of how I talk and that he wouldn't understand what that was like. For some reason that made him laugh even more.

We've decided that he's going to come to the carol service and I'll drive him home afterwards. That way he gets to meet the family, see the house, get over the horror of my choir robes and then if he wants to bail at Christmas we'll invent a sick granny or something. So a plan. For an idiot and an angel.

Dear Diary,

Christmas is a go! The carol concert was great.

Michael was really lovely, he was even more quiet than normal but everyone loved him. Especially when he started singing. His voice is so good and really deep, he's a proper bass and there he was booming out from the stalls rather than in the choir. We kept grinning at each other. Everyone standing around him raised their game and I've never heard the whole church sing so well. It was so perfect. Goldilocks led the school children in a perfect procession and the arrangement was spine-chilling. It was unaccompanied and they came in four separate processions, each holding a candle. Congregating in front of the choir stands for the final verse. That takes some real discipline, holding the tune when standing on your own without any accompanying music. I honestly thought it was going to be a disaster, but it was magical. I saw that Goldilocks had managed to wrap red tinsel around her white cuffs. Nothing too flashy but enough for everyone to note the difference. She'll go far. Afterwards at the Flint Hyssops people kept coming up to us and asking Michael if he was going to join the choir. He smiled and said he couldn't watch me sing if he was in the choir, so it was a no. Boy did I blush.

On the drive home Michael said he was a bit overwhelmed, but all in, meant all in. So he's coming!!!

Dear Diary,

Got my college report today. It was funny, it was a lot less detailed than my old school reports and a lot less personal but basically I'm doing very well. Showed it to Mummy and Daddy who said they weren't surprised, which was lovely of them. David said I was wasting my time hanging around with terrorists. Sometimes I really hate David, that was a horrible thing to say.

Dear Diary,

Best Christmas Ever. Picked up Michael on the morning of Christmas Eve and we went for a walk around the estate and dropped into The George for some mulled wine. Later we played silly buggers seeing if we could shout to each other from our bedrooms. He's in the garden wing so there wasn't a chance. It was like that game where you throw a ball to each other taking a step back each time, instead, we started in the minstrel's gallery and stepped a room back each time. We each took turns to say, "I love you" and soon we were having to shout it. Then I couldn't hear him and the next thing is he comes running into the room and gives me a huge hug and tells me I was too far away. I think the staff think we are bonkers. The folks were out doing the rounds and David was collecting Cecily from the station so we had the place to ourselves.

Cecily's a bitch. At Christmas lunch she made a snide comment about Michael's dinner jacket, suggesting it looked borrowed. She knew it was borrowed because David had told her. I was so proud of him though he laughed rather than be embarrassed and said he didn't own one. Like he wasn't even uncomfortable, then he thanked David for the loan and suggested that he would have to take up rowing or eat more mince pies as it was a bit big on him. Not sure if he was having a subtle dig at David. I think he might have heard a few terrorist comments over the past few days. I hope not. I really want them to get on.

Presents were lovely but my favourite was a portrait of me that Michael had drawn. It really is incredible, it's a line drawing in the Renaissance style. I look incredible. You could see that Mummy and Daddy were also really surprised and impressed and said they would get it framed. He also did a painting of the house for them and said he would love to paint it again in summer when the flowers are in bloom. David made a quip about Michael making more money painting the inside of the house. Like he's no better than a decorator. Cecily sniggered. Mummy offered them some coffee. I think she was a bit embarrassed by their manners.

Yesterday was Boxing Day so when the others went to the hunt, Michael and I went for another walk and I showed him my favourite places around the estate. It hasn't snowed in days but everywhere is still white as it's been so cold. We kept playing dragons' breath and skating across some of the larger sections of the flooded fields. Everywhere the sound was muffled and crunchy and it felt like we were the only people in the world. Michael told me he has never loved anyone so much. I just wish it could be me and him together alone forever. I am the luckiest girl in the world. And now I'm exhausted – goodnight.

To be continued…

Christmas Playlist

https://open.spotify.com/playlist/0xpxKmWp033KNz1QIRj47F

3 SPRING

Dear Diary,

I don't normally pay much attention to politics. It all gets really gloomy and depressing. The news is awful, always talking about bombs and strikes and riots. It's horrible, I don't know why they can't report on nice things instead. Why is it always bad news, never good news? Some of the girls at school were really worried about a nuclear war. When I spoke to Daddy about it he said it would never happen and I wasn't to worry. His reasoning was that the Russians were crazy but not stupid. He said the real worry would be if the Irish ever got the bomb as they were both crazy and stupid and had an ingrained hatred of the British. I thought them setting off a bomb so close to their home might be a bit of an own goal. Daddy told me I didn't know what I was talking about and got a bit heated.

I'm sure he doesn't still think like this, and now

he's actually met Michael I'm sure he can see how lovely he is and not like other Irish people.

Dear Diary,

Oh dear. Decided to see what Daddy thought of the Irish these days. That did not go down well. Within seconds he was calling them all terrorists and said they were like Nelson Mandela. I've heard of him. He's in South Africa and is apparently a terrorist but he's in prison. At college, there were a bunch of students going around with a petition to get him released because they said he was a freedom fighter. I mentioned this to Daddy and he exploded. I mean I was glad we were no longer talking about how awful the Irish are, but I seemed to have jumped from the fire into the furnace. He then started shouting that he wasn't paying for me to go to college to have my head filled with that sort of rubbish. So I pointed out that it was a state college and he wasn't actually paying anything. Well, then he started really shouting and it was all a bit scary and Mummy came in and sent me out on some chores. Daddy can be so unfair, I was only trying to have a conversation and try to get him to see how lovely Michael is and suddenly we were talking about South African terrorists. Like Michael is somehow in the same league!

Dear Diary,

I know I should drop it when Mummy told me to, but I realise I don't actually know anything about the IRA or Nelson Mandela. Am going to investigate.

Dear Diary,

Great assignments today. It was like the whole college was alive, everyone was buzzing. We have been sent the details for our end-of-year exhibitions and everyone is full of ideas. Michael will obviously be doing a painting exhibition. Zandi will be taking part in the fashion show and has asked if I will model for her. Which of course I will. Really exciting! I'm going to compose a new piano score and have decided to show a Russian influence. Obviously, I won't mention that to Daddy in case he thinks I've turned into a Communist or something. The end-of-year shows sound really exciting and apparently lots of scouts come along to check out the rising stars. Norwich has a great reputation for producing really great artists and designers. I bet someone will spot how good Michael is straight away. He said he was doing something introspective. I said was that spelt G-L-O-O-M-Y? He laughed and told me he was going to kiss me until I stopped talking nonsense. So that was fun! God, I am so in love with him. Even when I write about him I miss him because it means he's not here beside me. Sometimes I think about something that happened last year, and the memory seems wrong, until I realise it's because Michael isn't in it.

Dear Diary,

Snuck off to Norwich City Library and had to ask a Librarian to help me because I didn't have a clue. I asked if I could work down in the basement in the Specials Collection. I love it down there but also I didn't want anyone to see me. I mean as if, but you know, just in case. I've had enough of Daddy exploding at me and I don't think he was joking about making me leave college.

Anyway, talk about an eye-opener. Nelson Mandela has been in prison for years and has no end date and he didn't even kill anyone! So then I started looking into it and discovered that South Africa is like America in the sixties: they still have segregation. Today! They call it apartheid but it's the same thing. And it's even worse than America because Africa is a black continent. I mean everyone from there is originally black. So the white people are actually the new people. They are essentially guests. I mean segregation is sooooooo wrong, and it's evil and cruel and wicked but it's also really bloody rude.

Dear Diary,

Went down to the greenhouse to see if there were any early blooms I could cut for my bedroom. Jim was in there, so I decided I would ask him about Mandela and he was brilliant. And he made me laugh. He said he didn't care what colour anyone's skin is, everyone's heart is the same colour. But he wasn't in any hurry to see anyone's actual heart. So long as they were kind and decent, that was enough for him. I told him he was really smart, and he laughed and said if he was so smart how come he was out digging compost in the greenhouse, rather than up in the big house with his feet up!

Dear Diary,

Bit of a bummer today. Annette was asking everyone what they were doing for reading week and Michael said he was going to visit friends in London. I'm gutted. I cancelled going skiing so that I could spend the week with him. I've never missed skiing and there's always a good buzz. Mummy and Daddy and the other oldies all go off and do their things and the rest of us pretty much ski and party for the whole week. I haven't seen some of them since last year and it's always a blast, but I didn't want to be away from Michael for that long. Now he won't be here anyway. And I can't change my mind because I told Mummy I wasn't going because I had fallen behind in my college work and needed the reading week to catch up. And then that caused a row because Mummy said it wasn't really that important and I should catch up with my nice friends. Like my new friends aren't nice or something. God life sucks at times. Now I'm going to be all on my own this half term so I suppose that I will do college work. Although I'm not behind. Honestly, when have I ever been behind? I swear Mummy thinks education is a hobby.

Dear Diary,

HAPPY DAYS! God, Michael and I laughed. Turns out he remembered me talking about how a large gang of families all go skiing together every year, so he made his own plans because he didn't want to spend a week here without ME! Talk about a pair of silly billies. So anyway, he's cancelled his plans and we have the whole week together! So happy! No skiing for me but next year I'm going to convince Michael to come with me, he'll love it.

Dear Diary,

Can't believe it's March already. Getting really bad at keeping this diary going. Spending so much time with the guys from college and of course with Michael. We had the most amazing half term, I should try to remember it's called reading week. Makes me look like a schoolgirl. Last night was our six-month anniversary. It's gone in a flash. I've never dated anyone for so long, this feels really serious and I'm so happy. Michael never fools around; he doesn't embarrass me or make me feel stupid. He honestly makes me feel like the most important person in the world. When I enter a room, he stops whatever it is he's doing and comes over and gives me a small kiss. Sometimes I see other girls leaning over him or laugh loudly when he's around but he completely ignores them. I mean he isn't rude, he's just friendly and polite. Last night he gave me a ring, it's an Irish ring called a Claddagh ring and you give it to your sweetheart. I put it on straightaway and will never take it off. Feel gutted that I only got him some more stuff for his painting. He gets really twitchy if I spend money on him, which is daft because I've got loads and he doesn't. I guess it's a pride thing. Playing the Valentine's mix tape we did for each other constantly. Going to wear it out!

Dear Diary,

Hmm, April. This really isn't on. I think I will try to do a weekly round-up and see if that will keep me on track. I realise I've been talking too much about Michael (like that's even possible) but not talking about the end-of-year show which really is taking up a huge amount of time.

Michael (sorry) is doing an art exhibition (obviously) and the theme is Hope and Despair. I asked him if Leonard Cohen would be on the speakers and razor blades available for all that wanted to slit their wrists? He laughed and dabbed my nose with paint and told me not to be cheeky. I'm his model for a lot of the pictures but he won't show me them. That's cool but maddening, at least I know he won't make me look ugly, he is so talented. The picture he did of me is framed in my bedroom. I offered to compose some music for his exhibition but he laughed again and asked me what I knew of despair? Which I suppose is fair. But I wanted to help. Being a muse/model doesn't seem very hands-on.

The great thing about this process is how much we are all helping each other. I am composing a piece of music for my own portfolio and Jules has asked if I can do something for him as well. Zandi has asked me to be a model in her fashion show, see there are some good things about being too tall and skinny. She says it's going to be a searing indictment into the consumer greed of the capitalistic imperialist regime. So that sounds like fun! I suspect there will be lots of zips involved. Zandi is very into zips right now. But not to use to zip things up with because that's reductionist. Obviously. She's using zips that don't work to draw attention to what a zip actually represents. I asked if she meant like Plato, and she said no, his designs were derivative. I think we may have been talking at cross purposes. I left it there. Zandi is lovely but sometimes she does get very passionate and worked up about things. You wouldn't normally think zips could provoke a political discussion of the downtrodden but you never know when she's going to suddenly launch off into one.

My piece of music will be for cello and piano.

And I've been inspired by Russian composers so will wrap in some of what I've been learning in my lessons. The cello is going to bring the yearning and the piano will provide the power. I'm wondering about a third instrument to offer a counterbalance.

Dear Diary,

Spent most of the weekend at Michael's which honestly is a bit of a dump, but he doesn't really like it at mine. To be fair, it's hard to get a bus to here, and the folks haven't exactly been welcoming. It's hard to put my finger on it but I don't think they like him much. They are always friendly and polite but they never go that extra inch. And they always talk about my other friends and exes and what they are up to and then remind me to get on with my homework. In front of him. It's funny the only time they ever remind me not to neglect my studies is when Michael is over. The other day he came over for lunch on Sunday and suddenly we were dressing for dinner. Since when? We never dress for dinner on a Sunday. Cecily was down with David and they didn't blink an eye like it was an everyday event. Of course, Michael had nothing suitable, so I sided with him and the two of us sat to the table in our jeans and t-shirts. Daddy said something snide about pretend rebels and asked me in future not to disrespect Cook's efforts. I did go and apologise to her later and she said I wasn't to say sorry at all. The only respect she cared about was an empty plate and as Michael had asked for seconds, and the recipe, she was content. I hope she didn't notice how much food Cecily left on her plate, who was making all sorts of silly comments about making sure she didn't let herself go. In fairness her dress was so tight she was nearly popping out over the top. I suspect that was deliberate.

Dear Diary,

Am getting really good at Russian, really enjoying it and immersing myself in the history of the country. What an incredible history they have. And their country is so large, it's hard to understand how they have always managed to hold it together. I know that they are total Communists but once they were almost European, clearly for all the wrong the Royal Family did, they were also a good influence on the culture. Not like today, where everything seems brutal. But maybe it was always brutal? Obviously, people are more important than art but I can't imagine a world without Tchaikovsky or Faberge. What has Soviet Russia produced?

Dear Diary,

Feeling flat and lonely today. Michael has a triple shift at his pub this weekend which is obviously great for him but I'm bored. Went for a bike ride over to the coast but it really was too chilly to swim. Wrote a few letters to friends but they are all away in uni leading their new lives. I think I'm feeling so flat because I got a letter from Claire and apparently I was a bit of a joke at the ski party. I'd chosen to stay at home and play with my "tasty terrorist" her words. Can't get over how incredibly unfair this is to Michael. And how mean it was for people to talk about me behind my back like that. Not really sure who my friends are these days. I don't 100% fit in with the college crowd and my old friends seem to be turning on me. Mummy and Daddy are treating Michael like a fad but they don't seem to understand how important he is to me. Honestly, sometimes I think he's the only one that matters.

Dear Diary,

Spent the day helping Jim prepare for the Spring Fair. He likes to enter all the categories, so I was helping him clean up the prize vegetables and flowers. By the end of the day I was so covered in sweat and earth that he said I could pass for an African myself. Very funny. It was really lovely to spend the day helping someone and watch them as they take such pride in their work, and well he might, he is forever winning prizes, and I swear his veg is the tastiest I have ever eaten. He grows some categories for size and others for taste; he says if you breed for size you lose the flavour, so he does both. And lots of flowers because the house always needs flowers, Mummy insists that every room should always have fresh flowers in it. In winter we have lots of Japanese twig arrangements. Apparently, that's called ikebana, but Daddy and I just call it the season of dead sticks. I do like it when Daddy and I can have a bit of fun together. It doesn't happen often, David is clearly his favourite. No one even denies it. I don't mind but I think he's also Mummy's favourite. I think that staff like me more but that's small comfort. I know Mummy and Daddy are expecting me to marry someone really rich so that they don't have to worry about me not inheriting the estate. But that just isn't going to happen unless Michael wins on Ernie. And I bet he doesn't even have any premium bonds. He'll just have to become the world's best artist instead.

Dear Diary,

Had my first "fitting" for Zandi's outfits. Oh dear God. I am wearing a tiara, with dolls heads where the jewel drops would go, and my ball gown is made of bin bags. Just bin bags! Actually, it's pretty incredible and she has clearly put so much work into it. I am terrified that I will screw it up when I go down the catwalk. She says I have to learn to stop smiling. It's important that I look really stuck up. I'm going to pretend I'm Cecily, without the boobs! My skirt is really puffy with a big gathered puffy train. It's actually incredible to think that it's just bin bags. She says she has one more thing to do, but it's a secret. I tried to get her to tell me but she said she doesn't want to say anything in case she can't pull it off. I have to be the last person to walk on the catwalk for it to work. Nervous.

Dear Diary,

Jim won three gold rosettes at the spring fair. So pleased for him. Bought him a bottle of cider. He doesn't strike me as the wine sort.

Dear Diary,

End of term is racing to meet us. To be honest, I was having mixed feelings because it would mean I wouldn't see as much of Michael over the summer hols but he's had a brilliant idea. We're going to go Interrailing. How exciting is that?? I can barely contain myself. First, I had to convince my folks, that was not easy, then he had to come over and go through everything with them. It was like the Spanish Inquisition.

Mummy asked where we were going to sleep and I told her that that was the best bit, Europe has loads of overnight trains so we could actually sleep on the train and save on hotel bills. Boy was that a mistake! After quite a lot of words from Mummy and Daddy, Michael said that he would make sure we stayed in a hostel or hotel every night. Which I think will be a total fag. I think sleeping on the train is a really smart idea. In the end, they said I could go but only on the condition that I phone them EVERY day. Ugh. However, I can't complain. They've said yes and bought me loads of phone cards, set up a credit card for me and drawn out loads of travellers' cheques as well. At this rate, I'll be spending every night in a Hilton. I've told Michael about all the extra reserves but he says we'll be fine with the budget he first proposed. We'll keep all the extra stuff in case of emergencies. That seems like a good compromise to me. I can't wait. Honestly so excited, tomorrow, after rehearsals, we're going to the library and start to look at maps and see where we fancy going. Imagine a whole month together exploring Europe!

Dear Diary,

Zandi's idea for the end of the fashion show is inspired. Her tutor has approved it so it's on. I am going to trail blood from my fingers as I walk along. It's going to be amazing. Kevin has rigged up a contraption of fake blood bags and tubes that I will wear under the dress, and as I start walking, I will open the tubes and then drain out the blood. Apparently, I'm going to represent corporate corruption, blood of the innocents etc. Zandi's boyfriend is a hunt sab which has really put me off him but he sure knows his way around fake blood and violent protests. On reflection, not inviting Mummy and Daddy.

Dear Diary,

Been practising the best way to release the blood, we've been out on one of the parks trying to work it all out, obviously can't do it in the dress as it's too fragile for outside wear, and can't test the fake blood indoors as it makes too much of a mess. Got shouted at by the park keeper because we'd made his lovely lawn look like a crime scene. Felt really guilty, went back and left a tin of chocolates and a card to say sorry. Left it by the parks shed. Too much of a chicken to go and find him. Also, Kev called him some really rude names as we ran off so don't want to be associated with that sort of language.

Dear Diary,

Performed in St Peter Mancrofts. Such an honour. Everyone in the music department was really buzzing. The talent was amazing, even Mummy and Daddy agreed. To celebrate, they took Michael and me out for dinner at Tatler's afterwards. Mummy said I was the best, but it wasn't a competition, and honestly, I wasn't. I was good, but some of the compositions were breathtaking and the playing utterly exquisite. I was nearly crying listening to Han play the cello section in my composition. He elevated it so much, and I was really pleased to add a fiddle as well. I know it was irregular, but I wanted a sense of the Russian serfs as well as the aristocracy. I've been a real fan of Bartok, gathering all the original folk music. We tend to ignore and overlook the artistic outpouring of the masses and there is such beauty and talent there. Listen to me. I sound like Zandi. Anyway, I think I'm on for a B+ but an A would be amazing. Daddy was relieved that I didn't sound like the piece of rubbish (his words) that opened the show. I had to explain that it was incredibly clever and modern but I privately agree with him. I just don't get the current trend for atonal discordant noise. I have to call it noise. I really can't call it music. Tomorrow the art exhibition opens and will be showing in the Castle Gallery for a week. No idea what to wear. Gallery openings are usually really all about dressing up, but not with this lot. I'll follow Michael's lead, and pack a couple of outfits just in case. Really great night. Fabulous food and really exhausted that it's now all over. The folks aren't coming to Michael's exhibition. They have a bridge game they can't / won't cancel. And they don't know about the fashion show. So, bullet dodged there.

Dear Diary,

The last two days have been bonkers. Michael's exhibition actually made me cry. I got to see the pictures before the doors were opened which is just as well because I'd have looked distinctly stupid blubbing in front of the guests. He is just so talented that I am staggered. I mean I knew he was good but wow. Basically, the pictures were of people in really horrible places, none of the people look crushed. It's really hard to explain. One of the pictures has a grandfather standing in the ruins of a bombed-out building, the buildings are in shades of grey and really awful looking. The grandfather is almost superimposed, where the painting of the background is rough, the man is detailed and full of colour, and in it, he's smiling as he puts out some food for birds. All the pictures have this sort of blend. I'm in a lot of them, always smiling sweetly or laughing, amongst some really brutal backdrops. Then there are two pictures side by side. One is clearly a scene from Northern Ireland; a terrace street was strewn with dead children and dead soldiers. It's heartbreaking. The other picture is a portrait of me, smiling, looking up from a book. It's really uncomfortable because I think it makes me look like I don't care. Michael said people would understand that he was saying that we need to find ways to continue, despite the misery. That it's the small things that keep us going and the hope that fills our spirits.

Obviously, the majority of people agreed with Michael because by the end of the evening every single piece had sold! His tutor said this was really rare but well deserved.

Then the following day was the fashion show. I was still really quite emotional from the art show. In the dress rehearsal, Kev suggested that as I got to the end of the catwalk, that someone should come up and throw a bucket of fake blood in my face. I really want to support Zandi but I was really worried that she was going to go along with that. Thankfully, she dismissed the idea as overkill. She said if I did my part that would be enough. No pressure then.

Anyway, we eventually got to the evening show and because we were on last, we got to see everyone else's works. Not sure cardboard boxes for bras is going to catch on, and if we had one piece of military braiding, we had the whole Hussar regiment. Clearly, this is the year of zips, rips and military brocade.

Finally, it was Zandi's turn and her pieces went out to enthusiastic applause. She has quite a following. Then it was my turn and something really weird happened. I think it was because I was so tired and overwrought from the past few months. Anyway. I walked out onto the platform in my huge, glorious dress made of bin bags and my tiara with ripped-off dolls' heads. I tipped my nose up with a sneer on my face and stepped up onto the catwalk and surveyed the crowd with a superior air. Just like Zandi had said. I released the valves on the tubes and the blood started to pour. I could hear gasps in the audience and then suddenly I was totally overwhelmed, and I started to cry. I just couldn't stop myself. I started to walk, what else could I do?

So there I was walking and looking imperiously out at the crowd. I wasn't making a sound, but I was also blind with tears and gulping and trying to catch my breath. My mascara was running down my face and as I tried to wipe the tears away, I realised I was smearing blood all over my face. I got to the end of the catwalk with blood, tears and mascara running down my face whilst I looked out over the auditorium, cameras bulbs flashing in silence. You could have heard a pin drop. I turned and walked back carefully, my train smearing through the blood. As I stepped off behind the scenes, the audience erupted. I broke into huge noisy messy sobs and suddenly Michael was beside me hugging me and kissing me until he was also covered in blood and mascara. That made me laugh and then I was finally able to get a grip. Zandi said it was amazing, but when she suggested we all go out and celebrate I pleaded a headache. Michael wanted to come home with me and I told him I was really fine just very tired. Eventually, I convinced him that I was fine, and I went to my car on my own. Then I sat in the car and bawled my head off for about half an hour. Actually, it was quite scary, I don't know what brought that on. Slept most of the next day.

Dear Diary,

The last week has been a nightmare. Apparently, the show was being filmed, because it always is, by the Visual Arts department. They sold the footage to a local news crew that wanted to talk about Zandi as a new up-and-coming designer. Which is amazing exposure for her but one of the journalists decided to write a few words about me, and someone tipped them off about Michael's exhibition. Which has also resulted in some fabulous coverage for him, but the journalist started to dig into who I was and then suddenly they were off and running about Lady Elizabeth de Foix, only daughter of the ninth Earl of Hiverton, in a fashion show denouncing a capitalist society and posing in pictures about IRA violence. It's been incredibly horrible. There were journalists at the house and Daddy called the police to run them off for trespassing. I tried one day of college and everyone was pointing at me and whispering about me. Then a camera crew turned up and I legged it back home with

Michael by my side. He's been incredible. He removed all the art featuring me and told the buyers that they were no longer for sale.

Michael has been staying here, Daddy says if he's in his flat the press will just keep trying to mob him for a story. They also offered to pay him for the pictures that he withdrew which offended him. Then David said it was his bloody fault all this had happened, and he had no right to be offended. Oh yes. David came home. I was in The Telegraph and the Mail. David said I was a disgrace. Thank god Mummy has been on my side. Although when the others weren't around, she told me I had shown really poor judgement and that she was very disappointed in me.

I feel so wretched. I feel like I've been crying forever.

Dear Diary,

I think the piece in The Telegraph was the final straw for Daddy so we are off Interrailing today! He arranged both our tickets, our ferry crossing and the first night's accommodation in Paris. Separate rooms of course. And he glared at Michael when he said this. Charles, the local vet, is driving us to the ferry; we'll hide in the back of his Range Rover as we pass the press pack. Michael went with Cook yesterday, again hiding in her back seat, to collect his passport and rucksack from his digs in Norwich. So that's it. I'm all packed and whilst it's a huge rush, I absolutely cannot wait to escape.

Allons-y!

To be continued…

Sweet Valentine Mix Tape

https://open.spotify.com/playlist/13t1Bvkd5NdMv2kKYydCyb

4 SUMMER

Dear Diary,

First night in Paris.

We had our first fight today over a rucksack. Good to fall out over the big stuff. Actually, funnily enough, it was over the big stuff. Before we set out Michael had insisted that my suitcase was no good. Which annoyed Mummy because it's a Louis Vuitton. Michael said he didn't care who I'd borrowed it from it wasn't suitable for Inter-railing. I don't think Mummy had grasped how often I would be carrying my own bags. In fairness neither did I but Daddy agreed with Michael that it might make more sense if I had something a little easier to carry and a little less eye-catching. So we went into town and picked out some bags. Michael has this huge thing that you could honestly carry half a house in. I tried something similar and even though I'm tall for a girl, it was monstrous and there was no way I was going to be able to carry it fully loaded so I got a much smaller one and decided to pack light.

Anyway, we were in the train station and Michael had said he would find out where the buses run from and left me with the bags. I thought a bus was silly, we didn't have far to go, so we'd get a cab instead, so I decided to carry our bags over to the taxi rank. Well, then I realised just how heavy his rucksack was. I had mine on my back with all the straps done up but I just couldn't lift his so I started to drag it along the floor when this really nice man came up and offered to help. We got chatting, and it turned out that he was also heading to our hotel. Anyway, all of a sudden Michael turns up, furious, and asked this man what the hell did he think he was doing. In English. And the chap was really surprised, apologised and disappeared.

So I told Michael he had been really rude. He told me I was an idiot to trust a total stranger with his bag and I said total strangers carry my bags all the time and he said only when you pay them and I said, well I said nothing because well, he had a point. Then I said I needed some fresh air and was going for a walk and he shouted "fine" back at me and that he would come with me. So I shouted back that it was really hard to storm off when someone follows you. And then I realised how stupid that sounded and laughed and thank God so did he. So I took my rucksack off and sat on it and he sat on his in the middle of the train station, God knows what people thought of us. And he apologised for losing it but he wished I was a little more street smart, and then I apologised for being thoughtless but also wished he could be a bit more trusting.

When we got to the hotel, the same chap was in the bar. Michael told me to stay with the bags and he went straight up to him. I couldn't hear what they said but there was lots of laughter and handshakes and waving of arms. Anyway, Michael said he was a top man and that he's apologised for being a tool and bought the man a drink. He was worried that the man was going to deck him. Why on earth would he do that? And also very relieved that he spoke perfect English. Well dur. Although Michael obviously charmed him, most French people I know speak perfect English, they just refuse to do it.

Dear Diary,

Yesterday was quite a day. Still in Paris. As promised Daddy had booked us separate rooms but also on separate floors! Michael said he wasn't having that, he is uber overprotective at the moment. I'll come on to that. So anyway, he grabbed some sheets from his bed and made up a bed on the room's sofa. I pointed out that I had a double bed and what he said was incredible. He said, and I quote, "Way too much temptation" so I laughed and said that was sort of the point (I know, I'm a hussy) and he said that he was going to spend the rest of his life with me and there was no need to rush. Well, I was a bit speechless after that. And he looked all worried and asked if he had come on too strong and I was laughing or crying or I don't know what actually, but we made out for a bit and then he told me he was having a shower and then we were going to go and explore the city.

Anyway just out for day two. We have two more nights here so when we went down to breakfast

I explained to the concierge that Michael was unhappy being too far away from me so could we have adjoining rooms, as he didn't sleep well on the sofa. Just had breakfast so when we get back hopefully it will be all fixed. The concierge was really sweet about it.

Dear Diary,

Been teaching Michael basic French, he only speaks Russian which is really impressive but not very useful at the moment. Not being able to communicate with anyone has been making him a bit twitchy I think, and that's sort of making him feel more isolated and protective. I like it that he's feeling protective but not that he's feeling insecure. I told him a few words, a positive attitude, his gorgeous accent and that smile of his, wow that smile, and he'll be fine whichever country we're in.

Dear Diary,

Very excited. Our Inter-railing ticket starts today and we are off! For me, it feels like the adventure starts now. We are taking the fast train down to Spain and then straight on over into Morocco! Never been, very excited. We're also going to be sleeping on a night train but in chairs to save money.

Taught Michael Crib, he whipped me. Not fair. Beat him at Kings. Got chatting to a pair from Holland they taught us a great game called Cravat, I think? Takes two packs.

They got off in France, we're still heading for Madrid where we swap trains for a slow overnight to

Algeciras. From there we will take a ferry across the water.

Finished Hotel New Hampshire. Brilliant. Am going to run out of books.

Dear Diary,

I thought I'd have more time to write but we're too busy playing cards, reading, sleeping and EXPLORING! Morocco was just incredible. Totally and utterly like nothing else I've ever experienced. Very alien. When we arrived, I wanted to leave straight away. There were no women anywhere in the port or train station and all the men kept staring at me and banging into Michael. One even spat at the floor in front of us. I'd read the guidebooks, so I was in long sleeves and trousers but it was just too hot for a headscarf. After he spat at us I put the scarf on, it didn't help. Maybe they don't appreciate Hermes when they see it? Took it off again, too hot. A group of Liverpudlians came over to us and started speaking in French, asking for help. Very funny, even funnier when I started speaking in English and when they heard Michaels accent they were, as they put it, "made up". They were struggling as well with the natives so we decided to travel to Marrakesh together. Marrakesh is a much more chilled place. Love it. We stayed in a really old quarter and hired a guide to take us around the warren. Miles of tiny little passageways where people live and shop and play. No roads, just these tiny twisting little lanes lined with sand. Michael was worried about wasting money on a guide. I pointed out it was probably a pound for the whole day.

Learning bits of Arabic reminds me of Welsh, lots of stuff going on in the throat. When you walk around the street all the beggars (so many) hanging around listening to you to work out your nationality, then they greet you in your own tongue. So clever, kids under ten fluent in so many languages. Well, fluent enough to try and sell you something. In the end we switched to Russian and got a bit of space. Michael is so gorgeous; he gave them some food and spare change and now we have a little tribe wherever we go. He also gives them piggybacks and plays What's the Time Mr Wolf. Me and the mothers just rolled our eyes, but it was sweet and one of the ladies offered me some of her lunch. No idea what it was, but it was delicious.

Our guide was equally friendly and invited us for dinner at his. It was incredible. Once again, wasn't sure what I was eating, but the flavour was wonderful. I think I may have actually eaten goat! I gave him Hotel New Hampshire to say thank you, apparently English books are hard to get hold of over here and he's trying to improve his English which I thought was pretty excellent. His name was Fuad – almost certainly spelt wrong so, Shokran Fuad (Thank you Fuad)

I wanted to stay the whole month but Michael said it was great but he'd never seen the rest of Europe, which is a fair point, so we are now back on the train heading to Granada and the Alhambra.

Dear Diary,

I love Spain. I must admit I thought it was all donkeys and straw hats, which was a bit ignorant of me, but here at Granada it's not touristy at all. Well not totally. The food is yummy, and it helps that I recognise most of it.

Michael is now up to speed language-wise, a few words and a big smile go a very long way. The Spaniards couldn't be friendlier but they are very macho and only speak to Michael. I feel a little invisible occasionally, which is an odd feeling. I also keep lapsing into Italian which, it turns out, isn't in the slightest bit helpful.

Took a packed lunch into the Alhambra and just wandered around the incredible palaces and gardens. This is the most beautiful palace I have ever seen. Which seems disloyal to Hampton, Windsor and Westminster but this place seems to have been built out of flowers, sunshine, swallows and water. Wherever I walked I saw the ghost of the little princess, Catherine of Aragon, running and skipping along the corridors. As the child of Isabella and Ferdinand she must have been absolutely adored by the courtiers. She'd have been so happy and indulged here. What must she have thought as she arrived in England? A cold and wet country, struggling from centuries of civil war, passed down to the second brother to be finally cast aside for a younger model. If she knew what lay ahead I image you would see her fingernails scratched along the marble benches as she tried to hang on.

For myself, I was just happy to lie on them, under the scent of the rose blossom, eat oranges and olives and read my book. I'm getting a really nice suntan. Michael seems a little pink. He says Irish skin isn't meant for sunshine.

Dear Diary,

We have to make a 3 am change in Marseille. That should be fun. Can barely keep my eyes open. Nothing else is open either, the world feels deserted.

Crib – holding my own. Winning at Kings. Michael's winning at Cravat, his reflexes are so fast.

Reading Riders by Jilly Cooper. I swear I recognise the twins. Great fun. Swapped with a backpacker for a bag of falafels – some sort of faggot but tastier and no onion gravy.

Michael's reading The Road to Wigan Pier. I read that, made me feel awkward.

Comfortable nights' sleep – zero. I would kill for a bed without cockroaches or a train with a sleeper berth. Stoically, having done boarding school and Michael having slept on the streets we both have reserves to draw on. Clearly, he has greater reserves but our dormitories were really harsh. I haven't mentioned that to him as I know he'll tell me I don't have a clue. Although he's reading this journal anyway so no doubt I'll know he's got to this bit when he throws it at me! He doesn't read my diaries normally but this is more of a travel journal.

Dear Diary,

One night on the Amalfi coast and then we are sprinting over to Brindisi to catch the ferry to Athens. This is exhausting. Michael said our finances are really good at the moment so we could sleep in a hotel if we wanted. Instead, I convinced him to hitch down the coast a bit and we could sleep on the beach. It would be really romantic. Heavenly. Woke up to some serious tutting from a beach vendor as everyone was setting up around us. Less deserted than I had guessed. Lots of really black, black-skinned men with yellow eyes shining out. I kept staring at them. They were wandering up and down the beach singing out "Coco fresca" so chilled coconut juice for breakfast. Michael also bought me a woven bracelet. Naturally, we were then plagued by every seller and his mother. Still a lovely chilled day on the beach and thank God for beach showers finally managed to get clean again.

Hitched to the closest train station which happily had a direct line to Brindisi so Greece here we come.

Dear Diary,

Slept on the bench on the ferry crossing coming over. Michael was nervous again like he was going over to France and Morocco. However, he's now decided that the Irish Sea must just be the worst sea crossing in the world. The Ionian is a doodle. Landed in the dark and the air was buzzing with cicadids and dust and thousands of years of history. Michael squeezed my hand. Something very special about Greece. Slept in the train station and then caught the first train into Athens itself. Initial impressions are deeply disappointing. The noise. The smell. The diseased dogs. Michael suggested we go to the Acropolis before everyone else woke up and it was glorious. It was like watching all my history books come alive. We lay on the rocks watching lizards scoot past. Gradually the sun made it unbearable, and we headed off to shelter under the olive trees. Want to go to Delphi. But we might have to hitch. Train network here isn't great.

Went off to get some drinks, came back to find Michael doing a roaring trade in sketches. He catches a likeness really quickly. He earnt a pair of shorts, two books, some money and lunch. What a great day! Got chased off by some policemen with guns who asked to see our licence. Said we couldn't sell stuff without a licence. I said we earnt shorts, books and lunch and they weren't happy but told us to leave without issuing a fine. Blimey! Chased by the rozzers in the cradle of civilisation. Thank God it wasn't the soldiers, they wear pompoms for God's sake! Exeunt pursued by pompoms. Wonder what Mrs Bains would make of that?!

Dear Diary,

It's been a few days but haven't felt like writing. Haven't felt like anything. Desperately trying not to ruin Michael's holiday but I feel heartbroken.

It all started when I spoke to Lucy. We'd been hoping to meet her, and I called to see if she could break out of school for the weekend and she dropped the bombshell. David's got married. Married! Apparently, it was a rush job whilst I was out of the country so that I wouldn't attract the paparazzi. I couldn't stop crying. Lucy was horrified that I didn't know. Michael ended the call and then tried to cheer me up but what could he say? I've ruined my brother's wedding. I didn't even know they were engaged. Poor Cecily, I mean I don't even like her but she must have wanted a big wedding. The following day I had calmed down and rang Mummy. She said I wasn't to feel bad about it but that I'd have probably wanted to bring Michael and that would have sent the wrong note. I got a little hysterical at that point.

That was last week. Michael has been incredible. I feel like my family is deeply ashamed of me. To the point that they waited 'til I had left the country and then held a family celebration without me. And they are blaming the person I love most in the world. I just don't understand how they could do this to me. If David and Cecily had waited a few months, no one would have cared what the little sister of the next Duke of Hiverton got up to. I'd be yesterday's chip papers. Or do they really loathe Michael so much?

Dear Diary,

My family can naff off. I'm on holiday and I'm going to have a good time. We are now in Venice and I've booked us into a really nice hotel just by the Rialto on Daddy's credit card. If I'm going to be an embarrassment, I'm going to be a costly one. Michael said he wasn't happy about doing that. I haven't told him that Mummy blames him and I'm not letting him read this diary anymore so he may have guessed. Anyway, in the end he relented I think simply because he wants me to be happy. We have a lovely apartment looking over a canal and the most sumptuous bath. Every time I feel guilty I just think about them planning this wedding without me being there.

Anyway. It's time to think about heading home as the train pass is almost out so I've been buying a few souvenirs. I've also bought Cecily a little crystal bonbon bowl as a wedding present and a lovely leather belt for David. I bought those out of my money. I don't know how I'll be able to look them in the eye. I wish I had never agreed to be in that fashion show.

Michael has fallen in love with risottos. They are so tasty but incredibly filling. I'm sticking with salads and having the odd forkful from his plate.

We spent today seeing how far we could walk without hitting water. Not far. We kept having to double back all the time, but by the end we had managed to get quite some distance from the hotel. Took a boat back as we were totally lost.

Venice is the most surreal city in the world. Michael spends all his time sketching and the Italians love him. He looks Italian himself. In Florence he made loads of money sketching tourists. No one ran us off. Italy loves artists. In fact, we got free board and lodging from a restaurant that hired him to sketch their patrons in the bar and I played the piano. Great fun. That was for three nights. They said they have never been busier as the word went out and everyone was booking a table just to get a sketch by the new Raphael. Michael was delighted. We have to come back here again he is loving the art galleries and the churches. He seems very at home here. He's even picking up the lingo quicker than I am. Also thrashing me at Crib. This will not do at all!

Dear Diary,

I have come to a huge decision. Enormous. I am going to ask Michael to marry me!!!! The last week has made me realise how much I love him. And also how worried he is about my family. I know he thinks I'm too good for him, which is beyond ridiculous. I want to spend the rest of my life with him. So I need to make the first move. Because I don't think he will. He's too respectful. And perfect. And probably scared.

I've booked a water taxi to take us over to the islands and asked the hotel to pack me a celebratory hamper and have bought a simple golden signet ring with a winged lion on it. I think it's perfect. Very nervous. What if he says no? What if I'm being an idiot? What if I offend him by making the first move? What if the reason we haven't made love is because he doesn't actually fancy me? Oh God, what if he pities me? Or is just after my money? OK, this is ridiculous. No wonder men normally do the proposing, this is terrifying.

Have postponed until tomorrow. Feeling sick. Michael thinks something is wrong.

Dear Diary,

I AM ENGAGED!!!! He loves me. LIFE IS WONDERFUL. Oh God, it was so funny! I dropped the ring box, burped, messed up my lines and knelt on a banana skin. Nothing was going right and Michael just kept grinning at me the whole time, like he knew what was going on, and then I realised that he must have snuck a look in my diary. Yesterday he was panicking that I was about to dump him, so he read the diary to prepare himself, and then read that I was going to propose. So then he had to pretend he hadn't! But he gave the game away by grinning too much. I think me kneeling on someone's old rubbish was the final straw. So I slipped over and he helped me up, sat me on the park bench and then HE went down on one knee and asked me to marry HIM! And of course I said yes!!! He turned my Claddagh ring around which apparently means engagement rather than friendship. And he loves the ring I bought him. I bought it on my card rather than my parents, so he was happy about that.

Spent the rest of the day laughing, we could have danced back across the water. When we got to the hotel, the concierge staff all clapped and there was a huge bunch of flowers and champagne from the hotel in the bedroom. It was incredible. And then when we went out to dinner at the little restaurant around the corner the waiters all cheered when we came in. The Venetians are so wonderful. They feel like the friendliest people in the world.

Dear Diary,

I am in love. That is all. So happy!!!

Dear Diary,

The last few days have been amazing. We decided to change our plans and stay in Venice for the last three days. We have been wandering around the churches and galleries. Michael says we should come back to Italy and stay for longer. I completely agree. Maybe for our honeymoon? That seems ridiculous even saying that. Maybe next year? We both agree we should finish our courses first.

Michael and I have talked and we've both suggested keeping the engagement quiet until I work out the lay of the land with my family. I wanted to just announce it but Michael said life might be a bit easier if we paused for a bit. Especially after David and Cecily's rushed wedding. Admittedly that's a very touchy subject right now. But he's probably right. As usual.

Finally beating him at Crib, he says he's too

distracted by my beauty. I said he's too soppy but secretly I'm fine with that. Obviously.

We are now travelling north, heading towards the end of our holiday and rushing towards a great new adventure. My life is so good. I know I ruined David's wedding and I feel ashamed about that but I do think they could have waited. I'm also sad that Mummy hasn't warmed to Michael yet (I told you to stop reading this!) but she will because he's the best human being in the whole wide world. (Give me a kiss when you read this bit.)

I have loved every country we visited, and every book that we read. I wasn't impressed with my dodgy tummy in Casablanca and missing the train in Marseilles and having to spend an entire day in a train station with beggars and pickpockets. Delphi was incredible, hitching in the back of a donkey cart was very funny, and I wish I'd kept a better diary but we literally just talked and laughed our way around Europe. There just wasn't time to write. I'll write the rest of it up when I get home as I won't be able to see Michael on a daily basis. Not happy about that one bit.

Looking forward to being back in my own bed though. And some different clothes. I have a great tan, can't wait to see the girls, my hair is also full of highlights from the sun. I think Caroline is still in the Seychelles and Lucy is still in Switzerland. But Annabelle and the others should be home. Maybe Michael and I can spend the summer visiting everyone.

Scrap that, Michael said he has to work. Boo. OK.

Dear Diary,

My family are such hypocrites. So, we got back to Norwich and Michael went to his flat. He wanted to come with me to face the family after David's wedding but I wanted to do this alone. When I called the house for a lift, no one was home, but Mrs Dickens said she would come and pick me up. She's also cooked me lamb chops and cauliflower cheese followed by trifle. She's so lovely. A little hurt that my folks weren't home to greet me so I think my face must have really fallen. Dickie was lovely and I asked how much trouble I was in. And get this. None of the rushed wedding had anything to do with me. Cecily is pregnant! Like I said, HYPOCRITES. They were just punishing me because they don't like Michael. I can't believe they would be so spiteful. They used my "bad" behaviour as a foil for bringing forward the wedding. To avoid the "scandal." Like when the baby turns up in nine months' time everyone will know anyway. I get the impression that Dickie likes Michael more than Cecily, although she's always so discreet. Anyway, she put the kettle on and we spent the afternoon talking about David's wedding and my holiday and how much I love Michael.

Dear Diary,

Mummy said I was being hysterical about David's wedding. She said it was just like me to try and make it all about me. Which I thought was a bit harsh because that's exactly what she told me. I'll never forget her saying they had to get married straightaway because I had brought all the press attention on the family. I mean she actually said that to me, and now she says that I'm making it all about me! Then she said that Cecily's "condition" was a private matter and had nothing to do with the wedding. Yes. OK. I believe you. She also told me not to mention it to anyone. Including Michael. Absolutely. Lips sealed. As if.

Felt really bad for Dickie; I saw her later, and she had red eyes like she'd been crying. She said it was hay fever, but she's been with us for years and never had hay fever before. Sometimes my mother can be a right b. i. t. c. h.

Dear Diary,

I can't believe last week I was in Italy with Michael. It feels like a thousand years ago. I feel really lost without him. We spent 30 days together for nearly every minute and now it's just me in Hiverton. I told him about Cecily's pregnancy and he said we should hold off mentioning the engagement until she's three months safe. Apparently, pregnancies are fragile in the first 12 weeks and he says we shouldn't do anything to rock the boat. It's killing me not to say anything but when he's right, he's right.

We went to the movies last night. Some mafia film. When I got home Daddy asked if I wasn't bored of Michael yet? I get the distinct impression that they had both hoped that a month's holiday with Michael would make me somehow tire of him. Lummey, did they get that wrong!

Dear Diary,

What a brilliant day. David and Cecily came back from their honeymoon and everyone was happy and no one was blaming me. In fact, David was even making jokes about me being notorious. No one mentioned my trip or Michael but for the sake of family unity, I let it go. Today was a day for building bridges. Cecily looks amazing, I'm not kidding she is actually glowing. She's even being nice, well as much as she can be. Being a married woman seems to have calmed her down, and of course now she is Lady Cecily and she is loving that. Her engagement ring, which she must have touched a thousand times, is a rock the size of an ice cube. I honestly felt a small twinge but when I looked at my little Claddagh ring, I realised that I was smiling just as much as Cecily. I can't wait to move it onto my left hand but it will do for now.

Being married also seems to suit David, he suddenly seems to have grown up. He's got a bit of a swagger going on like he's the most important person in the room. I mean even more than usual. But I don't care, he seems so happy, in fact, they all do. Or maybe that's the champagne. I can't wait to share my engagement, but for now this is about them. They're moving into the townhouse which sort of makes sense. Daddy got David a job working in one of the London banks, so he won't have to travel and Cecily isn't a fan of the countryside. She laughed and said, "No offence but it's dead here." God she's awful and so rude. But Mummy just laughed along. I mean it's going to be decades before David inherits the house so maybe by then she'll like the countryside more? I wonder if they'll offer me and Michael the castle? I wonder if he even likes Scotland. Or maybe one of the places in Cornwall? The light down there would be wonderful for Michael's painting.

Dear Diary,

Well, the cat is out of the bag and my life is like a second-rate penny dreadful. Daddy's credit card bill came through so he phoned the hotel in Venice to ask them what the charges were for. Which I could have justified but then they offered him their congratulations on our engagement. As he shouted at me and Mummy, it became clear that at first, he thought they were referring to David and Cecily and when he realised they meant me and Michael he felt really stupid for not knowing about it.

Mummy then started shouting at me and they both started saying some really vile things about Michael. Daddy then actually dragged me upstairs and locked me in my bedroom. I was screaming at this point.

Anyway, that was yesterday. My throat is raw from screaming and crying but I've stopped now. It won't help. Now I am silent.

Today I have been given an ultimatum. I was allowed out of my room. Still not allowed any food. Am starving. I had to stand in Daddy's study and listen as they sat there and told me what was going to happen. They have taken away my car keys, none of the staff are allowed to talk to me and I can only have one meal a day. I have to quit college I also have to promise to no longer see Michael and they are going to send me to stay with some of their friends in New Zealand for a year to learn equine management. It's positively Victorian. I said no. Then they said if I defied them they would disown me. Actually throw me out of the house, cut me out of the will. I was then sent back to my room. So here I sit waiting for a tray of food. I honestly have no idea what to do. I am numb.

Mixtape for Interrailing

https://open.spotify.com/playlist/0GRm0HVQhU5Hk2ei8TFXU1

5 A NEW LIFE

Dear Diary,

Michael came home from work today and gave me this notepad. He said it's been months since he saw me write anything, so I should take up my diary again. In a way too much has happened, but he has a point, maybe I should try. It's just, I think who I was, is dead, and there's no point in trying to hold on to her. Rotting corpses don't make for great companions.

Dear Diary,

Well, that wasn't a great start. Last entry was five days ago but I am so busy that I never seem to have the time to write. But let's try and bring this diary up to date. After my parents turning into a Victorian melodrama, I decided that I was going to choose Michael over them. I didn't tell them though, as I needed to get away without them making life even harder. I waited until everyone had gone out then I phoned the phone box on Michael's street until someone picked up. I begged them to knock on his door and suddenly there he was, talking to me. I couldn't stop crying and he said he was coming over, so I stopped crying pretty bloody sharpish. David beating Michael up would not have helped the situation. I asked him if he really wanted to marry me, even if I had no money whatsoever, and he just laughed and said he'd love me even more. We hung up and I started to pack.

I couldn't fit a lot in my rucksack, so I packed my suitcases as well and put all my really expensive dresses in there to sell later. I had to leave my books and diaries behind but packed all the jewellery and run of the mill clothes. Then I called a taxi and jumped in. I couldn't even say goodbye to the staff as I didn't want them to be involved in any way. Next, I dumped my bags at Michael's and went to the bank where I have my savings accounts. I moved everything into my chequing account. I think my parents had forgotten that since 18 they had no control over my money.

I spent the first night with Michael, terrified that my parents were going to come storming into Norwich and start a fight, but there was nothing. The following day I rang the house and Daddy answered the phone. He basically said I had made my choice then and hung up. At this point I still think he had forgotten that I had access to my own money.

Michael and I spent the day talking, and it became clear to me that choosing Michael meant that I was also going to have to give up my course. I had a good lump of money but really if this was to be my life I needed to start working. God, even writing this I can't believe how naïve I was. Like work is an easy choice. Back then I thought it was going to be so simple.

I told Michael how much money I had in minor inheritances from various grandparents and he said that with that sort of money we could buy a house. Which we did. In London! It's not big. In fact it's like a dolls house and it's in the poorest area of the East End but it's ours and no one knows us. There's plenty of work around so we have no mortgage and money coming in every week. The house is in my name as Michael said he didn't want anyone to accuse him of being after me for my money. What money?!

When we moved in I sent my parents my change of address details and was sent a reply from Mummy asking me not to contact them again. More tears. There have been a lot of tears. Tired now. Will write again tomorrow.

Dear Diary,

Or next week. I'm not as good at keeping a diary as I used to be. Also I forgot to mention that I am now Mrs Byrne. That's right Dear Reader. I married him! Which actually has been the one thing holding me together through all this. My lovely little Claddagh ring now shines brightly on my left hand. It was the quietest of weddings, we were married in a registry office and two strangers acted as our witnesses. I had a word with the local priest and he assured me it was all legal but that we could also have a church blessing which made me feel much happier. I think it did Michael as well. Neither of us is really religious, but it's nice to have friends in high places, keeping an eye out for you. Especially as we are quite so all alone.

Hmm. I seem to be moping, and looking back I think I've been doing that a lot these past few months. This was smart of Michael. Getting me to write stuff down makes me realise how introspective I've probably been. (Michael says that's not why, and I haven't been moping.)

Anyway time to be positive.

Dear Diary,

My life. My life is a total adventure. This is what my day is like. We wake up at 7 and try to get out of bed. (Sex is fun!) Sometimes there isn't time to have breakfast and then we both head out and catch busses to work. I'm a receptionist at an art gallery which is fabulous, lots of modern art so unlikely to bump into any of the old crowd. I applied for some other jobs but apparently as I can't type I can't do anything. I'd like a career but at the moment not sure what. So the woman at the temping agency, that's a place where you go to which tells you about all the jobs available, she said I was pretty and talked nicely so I should be a receptionist. Sometimes it's a bit brain dead and I think some of the artists are proper charlatans but I'm hoping I can use it as a way to introduce Michael to the gallery owners.

Michael works as a hospital porter, which he says is a great job as it reminds you to be grateful for what you've got. We both work every day and whoever gets home first cooks supper. In the evening we listen to the radio, play cards or go to gigs in the nearby pubs. On the weekends, if we have any energy, we head into town and go and visit the free exhibitions.

We don't have a lot of money; all my money went into this house but our wages put food on the table and clothes on our backs. So life is good.

Dear Diary,

Sunday morning seems a good time for me to write. Let me tell you about our home. The front door opens straight onto the staircase and a corridor. From the corridor is our sitting room and then behind that is our dining room, then a kitchen, then a bathroom. An actual bathroom right behind the kitchen, and then out into a yard. There's no garden but I think in the spring we are going to try and put in some containers or something to grow some flowers. We have to walk quite a distance if we want to see any plants. The city is very exciting but also sometimes it really is very, very ugly. I found myself in church the other day staring longingly at the lilies in the stain glass windows. Can you imagine?

Anyway, back to our home. The stairs are in the corridor and head up to three apparently good-sized bedrooms. Honestly, they are tiny. Also, there's no lav, if you want to go, you have to go downstairs and through the kitchen. How embarrassing if you have guests? I wonder how people manage. Happily we don't have guests, so it's not too much of a bother.

The street we live on is even more adventurous than the house. It's like living in the United Nations. Because this part of London is quite run down, the property is super cheap even though the houses are a good size. Apparently. Seriously, after the first day of the estate agents showing us around various houses I had to stop asking questions. It was just embarrassing.

So, anyway we live in a terrace house, all the houses are attached to each other along the entire length of the road, and the front door opens almost right onto the pavement. There's a little bit to put the bins on that the estate agent called a garden, until I started laughing. Which was rude of me but honestly I hadn't realised how much houses cost and how little I could get for my money. Michael fell in love with it, so that was that. The agent said we got a bargain because it needs redecorating throughout. Honestly it looks like no one has ever touched it. He also reckons we should rip all the old mouldings out, so then it was Michael's turn to laugh. At least we both agree that modern isn't for us. Well, in houses anyway.

Dear Diary,

Had to write this down straight away. A really funny thing happened today at work. Tarquin came in today (he's the owner, his name is Terry but apparently Tarquin is more fitting – I'm not sure who he's kidding). Anyway, he came in with a new piece of work called "Futility - Part 3." There's no Part 1 or 2, that's also part of the artwork – the absence darling, the absence. Anyway, "Futility – Part 3" is an empty wastepaper bin. That's it. The artist didn't even make it himself. I said to Tarquin that that didn't seem very creative, and he told me not to be so plebeian. Artists don't have to actually make stuff, they just have to "visualise the creation and concept." Then, after I came back from lunch, I found that Daisy had moved it to the back office and had put her orange peels in there. Tarquin hit the roof, it was very funny. Daisy was mortified. The artist saw what she had done, kissed her, and promptly placed it right in the centre of the gallery floor, peelings and all. Renamed it "Despair. 1.2.3." and doubled the price. My money is on that bin being back in the office next week.

Dear Diary,

Too funny. We had an open evening event at the gallery. We have these, once a month to showcase new work. The bin was still in the middle of the floor. It has red marker tape on the floor around it. The peelings are mouldy and beginning to attract flies and it is now entitled "Despair 1.2.3.4.5.6." for each day unsold. And blow me but someone actually bought it. For £100, I have to work all month to earn that.

Tarquin says all the smart money is in what he calls installation art. All the big banks want installation pieces. Going to bring in my picture of me that Michael painted and put it on my desk. Then if anyone notices I can give them our address. Maybe we can turn the back bedroom into a studio for him?

Dear Diary,

Tarquin loved my portrait and has commissioned Michael to do one of him that will hang on the wall! After babysitting the children across the way, Mrs Singh showed me how to do a bit of cooking. They are a really lovely family from India and they both work really hard. They both have two jobs and tend to work in shifts looking after the children. On Tuesdays and Thursdays they have a gap where she needs to go to work, and he hasn't got back yet. It's only thirty minutes and the children aren't babies but I noticed this was happening regularly. So, I offered to go and sit there until the next parent came home. It's really nice as it gives me something new to do and I read the children stories. Mrs Singh says this is very important that they learn to speak like me, which I think is silly, but the parents are really adamant about this. They won't even speak their own language in front of the children. I think that's sad. Anyway, we're reading Swallows and Amazons at the moment which is great fun. Each time they send me home with supper for me and Michael. And it's delicious. I haven't eaten much Indian food before but it's incredible and Michael loves it as well. Actually, I'm a rubbish cook so I think Michael loves me babysitting.

Dear Diary,

We spent the weekend converting the back bedroom into a studio for Michael and he has started to paint our neighbours as well as patients from work. He says he loves doing it so he doesn't care if he gets paid or not. Although he'd rather get paid. That said, there's a bunch of hippies squatting down at the other end of the road and he spent the day with them sketching. When he came home, he was carrying a crate of really decent red wine. Being a hippy clearly pays well. Michael says not paying any bills clearly pays better. He has a point but they are really friendly and often go down the street after the binmen picking up any litter.

Michael often pops into the other houses to do preliminary sketches. His portraits tend to be in classical style but with a modern setting. It's like seeing a renaissance prince standing by the kitchen sink. I think they are incredible. It's really helping us settle in with our neighbours. I don't really know what to say to them. They are all a lot older than us or have children. We're a bit unusual having a house at our age. Also we're one of the few white people here and at the start our neighbours were a bit suspicious about us. I think they thought we must be squatters or drug dealers and they don't have a lot of time for either.

Mrs Okereke, she's Nigerian, says the Lord don't love a sinner. She has a lot of opinions based on what the Lord thinks. The Lord apparently is her constant companion. Praise be. She says that a lot. She keeps inviting me to her church but I tend to go to the local Catholic one. She says she went there once, but it smelt funny. I said her Lord smelt more like goat curries and she roared with laughter and said she'd been wondering about me. I made another joke and she told me not to take the Lord's name in vain. I'm learning my way around her. She and her opinions are quick to anger but just as quick to forgive. She reminds me of my old nanny and it's oddly comforting.

Dear Diary,

Last night I was stuck in a riot. I have never been so scared in my life. Someone had piled a load of rubbish across the road and the bus driver couldn't get down it and he said everyone had to get off and walk. I started down the main road past the barricades, sofas and planks on bins. By the time I got to the next road there were overturned cars. Young men were throwing bins across the road and bricks into shop windows. Others had loudspeakers and were shouting through them. Alarms were going off. The air was full of noise and things being thrown. It looked like something out of a war zone. I started running down side-streets, I was so scared that I might get hit with something. It brought back all those memories of those drunks chasing after me in Norwich. All I could think, was that I would be late for babysitting. What if the riots were on my street as well, the children would be terrified. I took my shoes off because I couldn't run in heels and a skirt. It was getting darker, more and more people were coming out onto the streets and I could hear sirens from the main road. I just wanted to get home as fast as I could. By the time I got in I was nearly hysterical and Michael was so wonderful. He had got home an hour earlier; he goes to work in the opposite direction. Also, I didn't need to worry about the children as Mr Singh said he wasn't going to work. It was too dangerous to be the wrong colour out on the streets, with both the police and the rioters attacking anyone they didn't like the look of. Insanity is running loose. I feel like I am living in Yeat's nightmare.

Dear Diary,

Went into work this morning. If I don't work, I don't get paid. Michael and I had words about it but in the end he relented, but he wasn't at all happy. I think worried sick was a better description. When I got to the gallery Tarquin said he'd watched it on the news and it was very exciting. By lunchtime the BBC said riots were likely to happen again, so I asked if I could go home early and he agreed. Honestly, I think he only said yes so that he'd have something juicy to tell his friends over drinks. How his receptionist has to brave tanks and bombs to get to work. Well not exactly, but by the time Tarquin has finished embellishing his tale I may as well be leading the resistance. To be honest, exciting isn't the first word that springs to mind when I think of last night.

The bus didn't go the whole way again but as I walked through the streets, it was quiet. Ugly quiet. The streets had lots of smashed glass on them and broken furniture. Some windows had wooden boards up and there were a few burnt-out cars. Others, like me, were picking their way through the debris, desperate to get home to the safety of their front doors. I had my camera with me so took a few photos. It's hard to believe this is happening half a mile from where I live. Where children play hopscotch on the pavement and my neighbours teach me to cook. Where Michael plays a new 7" on the record player and we dance together or laugh when we get the words wrong.

Used up the whole film so I dropped it into our local chemist on our street. No smiles, no small talk, just a slip of paper and a suspicious glance. I don't know why they looked at me like that. Over the past 48 hours I wonder if I know anything about the people I live with.

Spoke to Michael about it and he said they were probably just scared and I'd misinterpreted it. There aren't many white faces around here. I said I didn't want people to be scared of me because of how I looked. He laughed and said try being black or brown. Or being white but talking with an Irish accent. Lots of people are scared at the moment.

Dear Diary,

Didn't go to work today. The riots were very bad last night. Lots of police on the streets in riot gear. Terrifying. Went out and took some more photos, I wanted to show people how scary the police can look. I know they are here to protect us but some of them were shouting really rude words at some of the people on the streets. I suppose they are scared as well, but it's even more terrifying to think of policemen being scared. The media have started to call it race riots, but I saw loads of white men throwing stuff at shop windows as well. Some are fighting together. Sure there are black people fighting white people but this is more about poverty and boredom. Mrs Singh was denouncing the rioters in the strongest of terms. As though they had to prove to someone that they weren't to be associated with rioters. Who on earth would think that? She's lovely. Mr Singh says the police are doing a good job. The squatters at the end of the roads say they are fascist scum. Took some more photos of my street to show how lovely it is and how lovely all the people are. Even when they don't all agree.

I don't know what the answer is. I don't know why some people are angry and others aren't.

Dear Diary,

Hello again. I am rubbish at this! Reading back over the last entry reminds me of how scary it all was. It took weeks to settle down. The riots only lasted a couple of days and then, as far as the TV and newspapers were concerned, it was all over and they went running after the next "exciting" story. For the rest of us it took weeks to feel safe out on the streets and I know some neighbourhoods are just a simmering mess. Some people who had their cars trashed lost their jobs. Some shops closed down because they couldn't afford the repairs and we all had to listen to the politicians refer to us as problem areas. Problem people in problem areas. Thanks.

A journalist came around to do a background exposé of life on the edge. Cheeky blighter actually said that to our faces and Michael was so incensed that he showed him the photos I had taken during the riots. He really liked them but only wanted to use the ones of the actual riots, not of the normal ones of our neighbourhood. Not on the edge enough I suppose. He was going to buy them and wanted to know more about me but I started to get nervous. The last time the media asked questions about me it was a bit of a 'mare. Michael clearly saw I was getting bothered and told the guy we'd changed our mind.

The money would have been nice though. Michael lost his job as a kitchen porter so now he's working on a building site. He's always tired and there isn't always work. He's starting to charge for his portraits now, which is fair enough but he says it takes the joy out of it. I wish the gallery would take him on but he just doesn't suit their style of art. I might have to take some of his stuff to Cork Street and see if anyone there is interested.

Dear Diary,

Great gig last night. The band was on fire and we sang the whole way home. Drank too much, spent the morning feeling quite poorly.

Dear Diary,

Might not have been the drink. Still feel poorly, think it might have been the goat curry. Too embarrassed to ask Mrs Okereke if anyone in her house was ill, in case it sounds like I'm accusing her of food poisoning.

Dear Diary,

I can't be pregnant. I'm only 21. I haven't done anything yet. Too embarrassed to go to the doctors. I can't be pregnant.

Dear Diary,

Turns out saying "I can't be pregnant" a lot doesn't actually make you not pregnant. So, I'm pregnant. Wow! Got a book out from the library. Couldn't read it, lots of awful pictures. Will try again and see if I can find one without pictures. Michael is over the bloody moon.

Told work. Tarquin was thrilled for me and then asked when I was going to give up work. What the hell? I can't afford to give up work. Although he has a point. How can I work with a baby? He also said I'd have to stop before people could see I was pregnant as it would put them off. What?! He said his clients weren't hippies. When I told Michael he completely agreed with Tarquin. Not that I'd put people off but that I shouldn't be working.

Dear Diary,

Big fight with Michael. The thing is, I'm a bit

unsettled about being pregnant. Unsettled? Off my face terrified. What the hell do I know about being pregnant? I've never even held a baby. None of my friends have been pregnant. Obviously. We have so few family members that there is hardly anyone in our generation. No one at work has children. Clearly they all lose their job as soon as that happens. And that's really unfair too. Why should I lose my job just because I'm going to get fat for a bit? And exactly what am I supposed to wear? I can't waste money on clothes that I will only wear for a few months and then never again. I want to go back to Venice with Michael, can we do that with a baby? OK, deep breath, see what I mean. A bit panicky.

So, the only person I know that has been pregnant is Mummy. I had vowed never to write again to them after that horrible letter, but I didn't plan on getting pregnant. I mean, we are taking precautions. Anyway. I wrote to her, telling her my news. Maybe this could be the bridge that we need to come home. I mean I don't want to actually come home. I do love it here. But I miss my old life and I'd like to visit. And I do miss Mummy and Daddy and even David. I don't miss Cecily but she's pregnant or she was. Gosh, I must be an auntie!!!!!! Damn. My little one could have cousins to play with. David and I always said we missed not having cousins. You see, I want my family to be whole again. Even if they were really rude to Michael. I can see it from their point of view now. It was all very sudden and they never really got a chance to know him.

Like I said, I wrote a letter. That was a fortnight ago. I guess I was getting twitchy about it because Michael was beginning to act really weird. He's barely been in the same room as me for more than a minute before making a lame excuse and leaving. My hormones are a mess, apparently this is normal and finally I burst out and asked him if he was leaving? Was I so ugly now? Had the fun worn off? And then he shouted the same thing back at me! Was I bored? Did I want to go home? Had I made a mistake? Had this all just been fun and games, a little rich girl playing at being poor? Then he stormed out of the house and I cried a lot. A bit later he came back in and it was clear that he had been crying a lot too. His face was so blotchy and the pair of us laughed about how awful the other looked. We sat hugging on the little sofa and he said he didn't want to hurt me. I said he could only hurt me if he left me, so we cried a bit more. Pathetic really. And then he handed me Mummy's letter.

He had seen it last week and recognised the stationery. He was worried that something bad must have happened, so he opened it and read it. I know. But he was worried about me and the baby.

Anyway, he realised that I must have written first without saying anything to him. Which hurt him but the worst of it was her actual reply. Basically, my baby is a mongrel. She actually wrote mongrel. I lost it at that point, I remember howling a lot and the neighbours knocking on the door. And Michael and Mrs Okereke putting me to bed. That was two days ago. I couldn't go into work yesterday as I had the worst headache ever. I went in today but Tarquin sent me home early. He said if I was going to keep being ill I may need to stop work sooner rather than later.

Great.

Dear Diary,

One week on. Lots of things in my life are getting sorted. I was really unhappy about losing my family but Mrs Jones at the corner shop told me sad mummies make for sad babies and I'm not having that. The hippies in the squat told me that life is a rainbow and that a new dawn is a new day and lots of peace and love. Which sounded pretty empty but also rather happy. So I'm also taking that on board, whatever that is. Several of the ladies on the street have told me they know all there is to know about pregnancy and raising children and I'm to come to them whenever I have a question. Some aren't even waiting for me to come to them. They come knocking on the door with special remedies and clothes. I feel like the street project. It's funny, there was me thinking I didn't know anyone who had ever had a baby and my street is absolutely full of children. My doctor has said I'm in excellent health, if a bit skinny. I said my neighbours were on that, they keep bringing me plates of food. It's very funny really. I've completely lost my appetite but Michael is having a whale of a time. At this rate he's going to need a new belt. Also still quite flat, this apparently is normal in younger mothers so I can still go into work. I tried one of Mrs Okereke's kaftan things but Tarquin asked if I had taken up weed, the whole ethnic thing was a step too far. It was rather jolly. Huge blocks of colour all over it. Oh well, back to cream cheesecloth dresses then.

But I'm not grumbling. This is my life. It's not what I expected, but it's not a bad one. The future is going to be amazing. How can it not be? We are going to have a brand-new human as part of it very soon. I can't wait to meet her. No, I don't know. I just do know. If that even makes sense.

As the hippies say, peace and love man, peace and love.

Mix Tape for New Starts

https://open.spotify.com/playlist/0Lg2qA5DPQfO9CapCsNUeN

6 TIME FLIES

Dear Diary,

How funny to find these old diaries after all this time. Why on earth didn't I keep up with them? Stupid question. Five babies. That will ruin the best-laid plans of anyone, let alone me and Michael. But still I regret that I didn't keep them up. So I'm going to start again. Or maybe keep a sort of memoir. A memoir! How grand.

So, it's been eighteen years. There's no way I can say everything that happened. Those first steps, those scabby knees, the gold stars, the first crushes, the fights. All unrecorded but not forgotten. Like the time the twins cut each other's hair off, or when Aster painted the sofa, or Clem put pennies down the drain to feed the sewer dragon. Then there was that time Aster corrected her teacher and was right! But still there will be those little bits of minutiae that will have gone. Never mind. I'm no Pepys, I don't even like cheese.

A quick recap. Ariana was born and we felt such incredible joy. Almost instantly she made our family complete. We hadn't even realised we were missing something until she arrived. And then boom. Family. Noisy, dirty, exhausted family. But family just the same. Just under two years later Clemantine turned up and dear God was that a shock. We just thought another baby would be half the work. You know, because we knew what we had to do and it would be easy. It's worth putting on the record that nothing Clemantine does is easy. That girl! Anyway, another year later and I got pregnant again. Well obviously babies are a blessing but we weren't expecting another blessing quite so soon. And whilst we were reeling from the shock of being pregnant again, I found out I was expecting twins. Twins!

We didn't have names for them but Michael kept singing "Nick knack paddy whack give a dog a bone" to make Clemantine and Ariana laugh. He would blow raspberries on everyone's tummies and tickle their toes and the girls would giggle and the babies would do what babies do. Which is basically leak. So anyway, Michael said we should call the twins Nick and Paddy, and I said over my dead body and in the end we agreed on Nicoletta and Patricia.

Four children under the age of five. My God, life was hell. We always used birth control but were staggeringly unlucky. Anyway, after that there was no sex for a while. But obviously we did because three years later Aster arrived. And whilst she was another total blessing, Michael went and got a vasectomy!

Five lovely little girls all under the age of eight. I think Michael would have loved a son, and so would

I, but honestly the odds seemed to be against us. Poor Michael, he's forever complaining that he is outnumbered but secretly, he loves it. The girls aren't really into boyfriends yet but God help those poor lads when they do come knocking at the door.

Michael is planning to play up his accent and tell the boys that he knows "people" back home. The poor girls will never bring a lad to the house in case the IRA come for them!

During those years we did struggle. I couldn't work but I did do babysitting for others. I mean one more child wasn't going to make a difference in the Byrne nursery. I took in ironing and helped some of the local children with their homework and gave piano lessons. It wasn't a lot of money but it all helped. Michael took on two jobs, over the years he's worked on building sites, on the bins, hospital work, bar work. Whatever, whenever, wherever. Anything to keep the pennies rolling in faster than they rolled out.

OK. More later. My hand is getting cramped.

Dear Diary,

Well, there we were, seven of us in this little house. Thank God we'd had the foresight to buy the biggest house we could. And whilst some people thought we were living in the worst place in London, our neighbours were our saviours. I have never known such a lovely group of people. I am honoured to live here with them.

In the early days Vy used to bring around leftovers from her Sunday services. That helped set us up for the week. Sometimes Michael and I would have a large breakfast on the weekends and then not eat again until Monday. On Wednesday Mrs Singh would have some extra rice from her community evening. I tell you what, poverty is great for keeping your figure in check after childbirth. I used to walk everywhere pushing a buggy and eating sporadically. It also meant that I could return to my clothes without having to buy new ones. I only needed to replace them when they finally fell apart. I used to love shopping in Woolies in my old Balenciaga.

Again the ladies on the street were wonderful helping me learn how to sew.

Actually, writing this, I realise that I have been an utter fool. It wasn't an accident. They didn't have leftovers, every single week. They were deliberately helping us out. My God, how did I miss this? Those lovely, lovely ladies. I shall have to do something for them all to say thank you. Wait 'til I tell Michael. If he doesn't already know. I'm groaning as I write this. Of course he did! How blinkered was I?

I thought we were holding it together (just) but our neighbours must have seen how we were struggling. Well, I'm embarrassed. All those years of receiving charity.

Dear Diary,

Reading yesterday's entry back it all sounds a bit boo-hoo poor us. But honestly it's been mostly great. Certainly we've had struggles and the girls would have loved us to have a TV but we haven't really missed out. We have a piano; there were some hippies squatting down the road and when they moved out, the developers were throwing the piano away. It was only an upright but several of the men rolled it down the street and lifted it into our drawing room / front room. Michael drew a portrait for a piano tuner and we got it re-tuned for free. So much of our life has been about bartering. It's been fabulous.

All the girls can play, but Clemantine is extremely talented at it. She can also play upside down, which delights Aster. Nick and Paddy unsurprisingly are great at duets although they often turn into duels and one time they broke into a full-on fight pulling each other's hair out and falling on to the floor scratching and biting. God, they drive me insane at times. We also play board and card games and read a lot. All the girls have part-time jobs, except Aster as she's too young. That said she seems to be making money somehow and we haven't worked out how yet. She gives it to Clemantine to add to the weekly family hat. Every week we put all the money in the hat and then distribute some of it back to the girls as pocket money and use the rest for food and bills. Clem is bringing in the most money so maybe the girls think it's best to hide Aster's money there. Like we haven't noticed. At some point we are going to have to find out how she's doing it but honestly with Aster, I dread to think what we'll discover.

As this is turning more into a journal than a diary I think I should take a bit of time to describe the girls. Our wonderful, beautiful, amazing, gorgeous daughters.

Ariana

We had so much fun when Ariana was born. Of course, we didn't have a clue but suddenly her arrival made every sacrifice worthwhile. We would look at her, then look at each other and we didn't need to say a thing. Both of us knew in a heartbeat that we would give our lives for this tiny pink bundle of nappies and gurgles. It's hard to imagine such an elegant young lady as such a chubby, leaky baby but there we are. I named her Ariana after a distant Great Aunt and I've always admired the name. Michael felt it was a bit out of keeping with our current life so he would shorten it to Ari. And, as you will see, that was the naming pattern for all the girls.

We would walk her along in her buggy like Scarlett O'Hara and Rhett Butler. Michael would stop and show her off to every mother and would ask for their tips and opinions on how pretty she was and how to get her to sleep. And I would smile, tired and proud, and mentally take a note of everything they said. Although I had to laugh when one old granny told me I should pull all her teeth out as they come through. Teeth apparently being nothing but trouble. She grinned and gnashed her set at me. After that I also discounted all tips to put honey on the gums when she was teething.

Ari has grown up into a lovely happy girl. She has been my right hand in helping me with her sisters. Not that she's an angel. She loves going out to the local disco and sneaking in underage. Michael is getting ready to ground her for life. I've pointed out that she'll be off to university in a few weeks' time so we had better get used to it. He muttered darkly and then went quiet. I think we are all going to miss her ever so much. But Cambridge isn't too far away and she'll be home for Christmas. She reminds me of my mother from time to time. Tall and slim to the point of skinny, never clumsy, just naturally elegant. Michael laughs at how he could have created anything so calm. She's not one for boyfriends yet either, she has a little group of friends but she was the brightest girl in her school and that rather kept her apart from the rest of her year. Only one other child in her year is going on to university.

I'm so excited for her. She complains occasionally that she's not as pretty as her sisters and when I told her that she'll grow into her looks she burst into tears. So she may look outwardly calm and serene but really she is just like any other 18-year-old with the same hang ups and fears.

Clemantine

Chalk and cheese. Where Ari was quiet, Clem screamed. When Ari slept, Clem screamed. When Ari did her homework, Clem screamed. When Ari screamed, Clem screamed. Oh how Clem screamed. But, in fairness, when she wasn't screaming she was laughing or singing or jumping or dancing. She only calmed down about five years ago. She started to work with the Asian seamstresses. Mrs Singh asked her to help her sort buttons out. I think she took pity on me, the twins were having trouble with middle school and we were all exhausted. Clem hated school and was driving everyone insane. So Mrs Singh told her how important it was to get the right buttons in the right jars. Which she did and loved and asked for another task. Soon she was sewing the buttons on. She would sit so quietly as her needle punched in and out of the fine silks that it felt like a changeling had come in and swapped out Clemmie.

It didn't take long before her doodles started to have purpose and she began to design clothes. After a few years she actually began to make them. She earned money doing embroidery piece work and cutting work, and then she started to alter her sisters' clothes as well as mine. I think she has a great career ahead of her. If she can only get through school. But I seriously doubt that. She just can't get to grips with reading and writing, so school just makes her feel stupid. It's doubly hard for her as Ari is so damned bright. All through school, teachers would find out whose sister she was and instantly put her in the top set, where she would rapidly slide down to the bottom set, subject after subject. Except for art and sewing. Finally, a place to outshine her big sister.

Unsurprisingly, Clemantine is the party animal in the pack. She always has a thousand best friends on the go and when she isn't annoying people she's the life and soul of an event. She just won't learn to hold her peace. Teacher after teacher has learnt to their cost, that if they say something stupid, or pick on a student, that Clemantine will barge on in and give them her opinion. Unasked for, in front of the whole classroom and one time a whole assembly. She nearly got expelled for that one but how could we be cross with her for doing the right thing? I wish there were more people with her bravery.

She was the first one to have red hair, and I was quite shocked. Michael laughed and said she looked like a proper colleen. She was certainly a bonny baby and when she laughed, she would have the entire room laughing with her. She was so loud and so delightful. Even as a baby she wore her heart 100% on her sleeve. She's 16 now and still only five foot. The twins are already much taller than her and Aster, who's only ten, is about the same height. I know it bothers Clemantine but there's not much to be done about it. She wears high heels all the time except at school, where she carries a spare pair of flats in her satchel. She even jokes about making platform trainers. Nicoletta thought that was the dumbest thing going, she couldn't see how anyone would be able to run in them. Clemantine scoffed and said they wouldn't be for actually running in. Just for looking good in. See what I mean? What an imagination!

Nicoletta

Now honestly, I don't know who came first, Patricia or Nicoletta. It's on their birth certificate I guess but I asked not to be told and I didn't look. I wanted them to be their own persons, not because they were born first or second. During ante-natal there was so much rubbish about first twins being dominant, that I just thought that was pseudo self-defining clap trap, so I was determined not to play into that. Just like I've always tried to bring the girls up loving sports and maths and science. They all know how to change plugs and mend the fuse wires on the trip switches. They aren't wealthy, upper-class boys. So I have to make sure that they make the most out of every single other asset that they do have.

In the early days the twins were not a handful, no more than could be expected. I think even in their infancy they could see that Clemantine was hogging all the temper tantrums. They would bring me so much happiness. They were always smiling and laughing and would often both fall asleep at exactly the same time, often holding hands.

When they got to primary school, they began to make their differences from each other clear. Nicoletta seemed to feel a need to be separate more clearly than Patricia. It's hard to say if Nicoletta just looked at what her sister was like and then proceeded to do the opposite, or if she had her own natural talents. There was one time when Nicoletta hacked off her lovely long hair, she was about ten. Patricia took one look at her and promptly did the same. Nicoletta was so angry and Patricia was so unhappy. God, the tears. The following day Nicoletta got Michael's electric razor and shaved all her hair off. I think that was the breaking point for Patricia. From then on, they always had different hair styles.

Nicoletta, of all the girls, seems to have the most flair for the maths and sciences. She's also good at music and foreign languages, she and Patricia were always chatting away in Urdu. For ages I thought it was a special twin thing until a random stranger in a shop answered them. Boy, did I feel like an idiot. Mrs Bukhari, from down the road, thought it was very funny that I hadn't realised. Nicoletta also drops into a mean creole when her friends pop over. Back to the United Nations in our house. Apparently, her friends like our house because her mother doesn't spend all her time giving them the evils. I think I'm quite strict. Obviously not Nigerian or Indian strict. Jesus, those women think I am a pushover, although they did concede that for a white woman I'm the best they've seen. I don't think they are overly impressed with white discipline. At times I see where they are coming from. But honestly I leant all my lessons about how to be a mother from those lovely ladies.

Their children have such an impressive work ethic and always run their chores for the various aunties and uncles before they can do their own chores. I'm just not wired that way so we've struggled along. To the amused observance of our neighbours.

Patricia

Well if Nicoletta is all street and sharp, Patricia is a great big pile of goo. Pink was made for Princess Patricia. She can't see the wrong in anyone and spends her days playing with pretend ponies and dreaming of having a pet. There are days when I see her yearning so much for what I took for granted that I feel ashamed of myself. A few years back Patricia heard about a city farm through school and saved up her paper round money for the bus fare after school. We got a phone call from the farm asking us if we could collect her. She now spends every Saturday there, mucking out the animals and riding the horses at the end of the day.

Of all the girls I suppose I'm the most worried about her. I think all the girls are beautiful but she is stunning. Even at fourteen, grown men are turning to look at her. And she has the most trusting nature, all she wants to do is fall in love, be happy and ride ponies. It's not a bad dream is it? But the world she lives in isn't that nice to daydreamers.

Of course she will always have Nicoletta by her side. Despite her early desire to be seen as different from her twin, Nicoletta and Patricia have always been a unit. They are always the first to run to the defence of the other. At cards they always cheat to help the other one win, or grab the other's favourite Quality Street at Christmas before anyone else can get it, and we have long since given up on Monopoly.

Clemantine and Aster often shout at them for ganging up but most of the time the girls just take it for what it is. The other girls don't seem jealous and there are loads of times where it's Aster, Ariana and Patricia against Clemantine and Nicoletta. So they aren't exclusively twins, where no one else can join in. It's just that they are twins, and every now and then it's screamingly obvious. Looks wise it's clear they aren't identical. Patricia got the red hair and Nicoletta the dark hair. Like the others they are blue eyed and pale skinned, with freckles. But there's something about the arrangement of Patricia's features that make her incredibly beautiful, we were in town the other day and a talent scout came up to me and asked if she would be interested in modelling. Her height, slim frame and unusual look were considered editorial. I thanked them and pointed out she was only 14. Plus what I didn't say was that I thought a modelling career might be a really bad idea for such a trusting soul as her. Still, I've kept the card, it's an agency called Models One. I've looked them up on Yellow Pages and they seem genuine. But even so, Michael and I are wary. It's something to think about, although of course Patricia is now pestering us daily about it.

Aster

Our little shining star. Well, I may worry the most about Patricia but I have no idea what to make of Aster. None of us do. We never have.

As a little girl she would sit quietly amongst her sisters. She never begged them to join in or for them to include her. When they did, she loved it and played happily, and when they didn't, she seemed just as contented.

I often feel a bit guilty about her. She has an odd moral compass and is often overlooked. I worry that as a mother, I may too, have overlooked her. It was such a relief to have a child that didn't demand all my time and attention. She has had all my love. Quiet times with her have been some of my very favourite moments. She is so undemanding that it is a total joy to be in her company. But I worry that I could do more.

Her teachers say she is exceptionally bright, and they mentioned moving her up a year group. Michael and I aren't sure what to do, she says she doesn't care, but I'm worried that putting her up a year will isolate her from her age group and introduce her to teenage issues before she is ready. We don't want to hold her back but I think maybe another year? Sometimes she views the world a bit differently and I don't want to throw her another googly.

A few years back at Christmas, we all opened our presents. Normally, a modest affair but not that year. It seems that when we had gone into town to admire the lights, Aster had been happily shoplifting. She was only eight! We had gone through this issue of ownership and theft when she was smaller and had taught her that she couldn't just take things from the corner shops.

When she was very small, she would just take her sisters things or mine. This seemed totally normal to us, we just needed to explain ownership. I think then she simply didn't see a difference between her and the rest of the family. She had no sense of boundaries. When she was four or five, we realised it might not be a boundary issue as she started to help herself to items from the local shops. Thankfully (?) we were never publicly embarrassed as she seemed to get away with it but I noticed that she suddenly had things that I hadn't bought. Michael made her return everything and if she got caught returning it, then she would have to face her punishment from the shopkeeper. It was a tough punishment, but I understood what Michael was trying to instil. I think what she learnt though was how to be even more circumspect. She did ask us what she should do about the sweets she had eaten. She was so serious! In the end we tried to explain that you don't take from friends and that we should view our community around us as friends. Over the years I would catch her helping the various local shops bring in their deliveries or cleaning their windowsills. If she spotted someone stealing in the shop, she would shout loudly at them. I was always worried about this but she asked who would hurt a little kid like herself? It was the artless way that she asked made me realise that she was completely orchestrating the situation. She knows that she is small, even for her age, and she is using that to her advantage. That was one of those moments when I realised that Aster's mind is always calculating.

Anyway, then came the Christmas fiasco. The twins got gold bracelets, I got a silver picture frame, oh it was beautiful. Michael got a crocodile skin wallet, Ariana got a Hermes scarf and Clemantine got a paint set. It looked like she'd cleared out Liberty's. I was horrified. Michael was furious. When we challenged her, she said that we didn't know the people that owned Liberty's, so it was OK? We took an hour explaining in no uncertain terms that taking something from anyone, is wrong. In turn she quizzed us backwards and forwards.

Could she take something from someone who had already stolen that thing? Could she take something if it would save someone else's life? If it saved her life? What if she was starving, could she steal an apple? If a person were sleeping on the street could they steal a house? Is breaking into a house to sleep, stealing? When Gary copies her homework is that stealing?

By the end of it I was really sad. It was clear that Aster doesn't see the world the same way as the rest of us and I'm so worried. Michael says it will be OK. Once the rules are explained clearly to her, she does appear to follow them. My worry is that at some point in the future she will decide that the rules are wrong.

The girls thought it was funny, I think they had realised years before us that Aster was wired a bit differently and didn't care. They were less impressed when we told them they couldn't keep their presents. We donated them to charity. I was too scared to make her return them to Liberty's. Despite her assurance that she wouldn't get caught (she saw it as a challenge not a punishment) I was worried that the police would get involved. I mean it's Liberty's and God knows how much those gold bracelets cost. The funny thing was that the presents were all different prices. Clemantine's present was probably the cheapest by a long shot but it was perfect for her. Aster didn't care about the cost, just how perfect the gift was for the recipient. That's her upside, she loves her family so much and really understands us. She is very loving and very thoughtful. Which works for me, for now. What the future holds for her is a mystery but if I open the paper one day and find that she has led a military coup, and is now running a country, I don't think I would even blink.

So where are we today?

Ariana and Clemantine are waiting on their exam results. Top tip to any future parents, do not have children two years apart. Makes the revision, exams and results process doubly appalling. Ari I think is going to sail through, even though her place at Cambridge is unconditional, it will be nice for her to go in with her head high. Clemantine, I suspect, will do less well. She's clearly not stupid but there's something about her that just doesn't do exams. She doesn't even like reading in a household of avid readers. Clearly, her father's daughter.

Nicoletta, Patricia and Aster are all watching their older sisters with concern and a certain amount of anticipation. With Ariana gone, one of them will move into share with Clemantine. Three in one bedroom has always been a struggle. I'm sure they are going to miss Ariana, but having a bit more privacy will sure take the sting out of it!

Michael and I are off out for a gig tonight. It's our weekly treat to just have a bit of time for ourselves and listening to new bands. Our tastes in music are still close but there are some near misses. I love Kate Bush, he loves Dead Can Dance. He likes his music deep and solemn, I like it euphoric. We both agree that Bucks Fizz are dreadful. We take bets as we're walking to the venue about who's going to enjoy the gig more. Loser has to bring the other a cup of tea in bed in the morning. I love these little moments when it's just the two of us. He's still clearly the best-looking guy in the room and every time I see him my heart still skips a beat. The other day I came back from the cloakroom and saw a bunch of teenage girls giggling and chatting at the bar throwing him looks. Poor chap, he was desperately pretending that he couldn't see or hear them. I came and rescued him with a huge kiss and nicely told the girls that boys their own age were probably a better bet. Ah, the joys and terror of being a teenager.

Tomorrow I'll write more about what Michael and I are up to these days. There are some really exciting developments ahead! So looking forward to it.

Mix Tape for Now We Are Seven

https://open.spotify.com/playlist/6smNQ4T7eA8DFmTmicoW19

…

Clemmie's Note.

This is where her diaries end. We know the rest.

WHAT HAPPENS NEXT

Welcome to *A New Life for Ariana Byrne.* Set ten years after the diaries end, find out what happens to Lily and Michael's children.

What does a girl from a London sink estate know about being a Countess? Ari's about to find out!

She knows how to fight and how to survive. She knows how to take care of her sisters and her children but how on earth can she take care of an entire village? Can she fight off the circling land developers and stop her in-laws from grabbing all the money for themselves?

And while she's struggling to settle in and settle down, she's making new friends and new mistakes. Trusting her gorgeous neighbour may be the biggest one of all.

From a life of toil and drudgery to one of tractors and tiaras see how Ari pulls it off in this modern day rags to riches, feel-good story.

Be warned, this is one book that you won't want to put down.

Download now and treat yourself to this summer's feel-good blockbuster.

AVAILABLE NOW

https://books2read.com/u/3G2wBO

This is a Universal Link and will take you to your

preferred shop, anywhere in the world.

Readers are loving *A New Life for Ariana Byrne*!

'I had a **great big smile on my face** while reading…**Funny, feel-good and fabulous**, this is an exceptional tale fans of Katie Fforde and Jill Mansell are going to love…fantastic romantic comedy that **will make you giggle on many an occasion**.' *Bookish Jottings*

'This is **an absolutely perfect and gorgeous read.** I have loved every single page.…There is no way I can **give this book anything less than five stars**. It's been a joy to read.' *Little Miss Book Lover 87*

'I loved this book. I loved the characters, I loved that there were so many strong female personalities…**Everything about this novel was fab**' *Chapter and Cake*

'If you're looking for **a truly heartwarming story**, this has to be a top contender… I found it easy to escape into this lovely story and **have absolutely no hesitation in highly recommending it**.' *Splashes Into Books*

'such an **uplifting, enjoyable page turner that it was a delight to read!...** Having characters as brilliant as these, with such phenomenal development, makes this rags to riches romance **a thoroughly enjoyable read**.' *Books and Bookends*

'Totally loved this book and read it in one day, even though it almost led to 24 hours without sleep just to finish it!' *Tizi's Book Reviews*

'The book was **a pleasure to read**, it had

some lovely characters and I really enjoyed the setting of the book too…**It is 5 stars from me for this one**…a heartfelt and lovely read – **very highly recommended!**' *Donna's Book Blog*

'The writing was **upbeat, funny and flowing**, all in all a strong debut…a great addition to the romantic comedy canon and **I really enjoyed it**.' *A Little Book Problem*

'It has **parts that make you laugh**, **parts that make you angry and sad**, and parts that make your **heart go pitter-patter!!!...**I felt like I was a part of the story myself!' *Devilishly Delicious Book Reviews*

'A **heartening, truly uplifting story**….Ari is **likeable, determined and genuine**….demonstrates both deftness of plot and great skill by the author' *Books Are Cool*

https://books2read.com/u/3G2wBO

WOULD YOU LIKE TO HELP?

Did you enjoy this book? You can make a big difference.

Reviews are very powerful and can help me build my audience. Independent authors have a much closer relationship with their readers, and we survive and thrive with your help.

If you've enjoyed this book, then please let others know.

The more good reviews I get, the more the algorithms notice and then promote my book for me. And you know nothing promotes books better than great feedback !

HELLO AND THANK YOU

Why not join my mailing list to keep up to date with new releases, free excerpts, interviews and behind-the-scenes insights?

Getting to know my readers is really rewarding, I get to know more about you and enjoy your feedback; it only seems fair that you get something in return so if you sign up for my newsletter you will get various free downloads, depending on what I am currently working on, plus advance notice of new releases. I don't send out many newsletters, and I will never share your details. If this sounds good, click on the following: www.lizhurleywrites.com

Find out more on Facebook or Instagram

Printed in Great Britain
by Amazon